THE TURNOVER

ALSO BY MIKE LUPICA

THE TURNOVER

MIKE LUPICA

SIMON & SCHUSTER BOOKS FOR YOUNG READERS
NEW YORK LONDON TORONTO SYDNEY NEW DELHI

SIMON & SCHUSTER BOOKS FOR YOUNG READERS
An imprint of Simon & Schuster Children's Publishing Division
1230 Avenue of the Americas, New York, New York 10020

SIMON & SCHUSTER BOOKS FOR YOUNG READERS is a trademark of Simon & Schuster, Inc.
For information about special discounts for bulk purchases, please contact Simon & Schuster Special Sales at 1-866-506-1949 or business@simonandschuster.com.
The Simon & Schuster Speakers Bureau can bring authors to your live event. For more information or to book an event, contact the Simon & Schuster Speakers Bureau at 1-866-248-3049 or visit our website at www.simonspeakers.com.
Book design by Greg Stadnyk
The text for this book was set in Adobe Garmond Pro.
Manufactured in the United States of America
0420 FFG
First Edition
2 4 6 8 10 9 7 5 3 1
Library of Congress Cataloging-in-Publication Data
Names: Lupica, Mike, author.
Title: The turnover / Mike Lupica.
Description: First edition. | New York : Simon & Schuster Books for Young Readers, [2020] | Audience: Ages 8 to 12. | Audience: Grades 4–6. | Summary: "When a young basketball star decides to research his grandfather—and coach—for a school project, he uncovers a decades-old scandal that changes everything he thought he knew about his grandfather"— Provided by publisher.
Identifiers: LCCN 2019031128 (print) | LCCN 2019031129 (eBook) | ISBN 9781534421585 (hardcover) | ISBN 9781534421608 (pdf)
Subjects: CYAC: Basketball—Fiction. | Coaches (Athletics)—Fiction. | Grandfathers—Fiction. | Scandals—Fiction.
Classification: LCC PZ7.L97914 Tur 2020 (print) | LCC PZ7.L97914 (eBook) | DDC [Fic]—dc23
LC record available at https://lccn.loc.gov/2019031128
LC eBook record available at https://lccn.loc.gov/2019031129

This book is for the great Esther Newberg.

THE TURNOVER

ONE

Lucas Winston loved basketball the most when it was just him and Gramps in the park.

He also loved being on the seventh-grade town team in Claremont. He loved playing in the Twin Lakes League season, against all the other town teams in their area. He loved the fact that his sixth-grade team had won the Twin Lakes championship last year. And he sure didn't hate that his best friend, Ryan Moretti, was the most gifted big man in the league, and a player who knew what to do with the ball when Lucas passed it to him.

"No two boys your age ever ran the pick-and-roll better," Gramps said to Lucas one time.

Gramps had a way of making almost anything into the best he'd ever seen or known, starting with the French toast he'd had for breakfast that morning at the Claremont Diner.

"Trust me," Gramps said. "You know how they say, 'Ball don't lie'? When it comes to analyzing basketball, I don't either."

"I know," Lucas said. "Nobody knows more about basketball than you do."

Last year Sam Winston had been the only grandfather coaching in the Twin Lakes League, and the Claremont Wolves had won their first title since before Lucas was even born. The parents on the board of directors were so happy with the job he'd done, they asked him to come back and coach the seventh graders this season, even though he'd announced he was retiring.

Lucas never believed Gramps's heart was really in retiring. He knew he'd never stop loving basketball the way he did, and would always want to teach it. So Lucas had been the one to talk him out of it.

At the time he said to his grandfather, "You and I are the best team in town. And I'm not letting you break up *that* team."

Lucas believed it too. He knew Gramps had taught him as much about being a good teammate as he had about being a good point guard. Persuading Gramps to come back was just one more way of being the best teammate he could be.

Lucas's grandfather was really the only *father* Lucas had ever known. His real father had died of cancer right after Lucas was born. So they had always been a team, and not just in basketball. Sam Winston had never been too busy for Lucas, even before he'd retired from driving a USPS truck and delivering the mail.

It wasn't too cold tonight under the lights at Westley Park. Tryouts were over for this year's Wolves. The roster had been set. Their first game, against Homestead, was scheduled for next Saturday morning, in the new gym at Claremont Middle School.

Lucas and Gramps were working on what his grandfather called "old-school stuff."

"Which some people would probably call 'old-man stuff,'" Sam Winston said.

"But you always tell me that the fundamentals never get old," Lucas said.

"You just have to adapt them to the times," Gramps said. He smiled. With his white hair and white beard, when he smiled he always reminded Lucas a little bit of Santa Claus. "You know I didn't like the three-point shot when they first shoved it down my throat. And I can't say as I *love* it even now. But I'm smart enough to know that if all you do is look back, you're going to get left behind, no matter how much you love the game."

They were both dressed in hoodies and sweatpants. Gramps was wearing one with USPS on the front. Lucas was wearing the purple Lakers hoodie that Gramps had bought him to replace the one from the Cavs he'd given Lucas when LeBron James was still playing in Cleveland. LeBron, even though he was the one getting older now, was Gramps's favorite out of all the modern NBA players. He'd become one of Lucas's favorites too.

Gramps said it wasn't LeBron's size or his strength that made him love LeBron's game so much. It was his unselfishness. It hadn't helped the Lakers very much in his first season in Los Angeles. But the point Gramps kept hitting with Lucas was that the best player in the NBA was also the best teammate.

"He never takes a shot if his teammate has a better one," Gramps said.

"My coach always tells me that's the first rule of offensive basketball," Lucas said, knowing he was about to quote Gramps *to* Gramps. "If you're open, shoot the darn ball. If you've got a teammate more open than you, pass it and let him shoot the darn ball. Or her."

Gramps smiled again.

"And who said that first," Gramps said, "even if nobody but me remembers?"

MIKE LUPICA

"Coach Red Auerbach of the Boston Celtics," Lucas said, feeling as if he were answering a question in class.

"And who was Red Auerbach?" Gramps said.

"The greatest NBA coach of all time," Lucas said. Now he smiled. "Even if Phil Jackson came along later to win more championships."

That was another thing Gramps was big on: having Lucas understand the history of the game. Looking back, he told Lucas, would help him understand how basketball had changed.

"I know people act as if those old Boston Celtics that Red coached played their home games at Jurassic Park," Gramps said. "But I'm going to tell you something right now: Red Auerbach loved Michael Jordan and he would have loved LeBron."

Lucas didn't care if his friends didn't love basketball history the way he did. Gramps cared; that's what mattered to him. And if he did, Lucas did.

Tonight at Westley Park the two of them had spent a fair amount of time working on the high pick-and-roll, which was so old school, Gramps joked he wasn't even sure they *had* schools when teams started using the play. Lucas and Ryan had run it all last season, and Gramps said they were going to wear teams out running it again this season.

Gramps said the truth was that if you started your offense

that way and ran it right, it didn't matter whether the other team knew it was coming or not.

Gramps was playing the part of Ryan tonight. Over and over he'd limp up to the top of the key on his aching knees, wincing as he did. Those knees, Lucas knew, were the oldest things about his grandfather. Not his mind. Not his attitude. Not even his heart. Just the knees. He never begged off playing. He never complained about his knees, even though Lucas could see the pain on his face when he'd move around a lot like this.

As soon as Gramps called for the ball, Lucas tossed it to him.

"Switch!" Gramps yelled, passing the ball to Lucas as he moved to his right.

It meant the imaginary player guarding him was jumping out to guard Lucas.

Lucas didn't hesitate as Gramps spun away from him and hobbled down the left side of the lane toward the basket. He lofted a pass over the smaller imaginary player who would have switched over to guard Gramps, hit Gramps perfectly in stride— if you could even call what his grandfather did *striding*—and Gramps put a left-handed layup off the backboard and gently through the net.

"Now that's what I'm talking about!" Sam Winston said.

"Did I get the pass away quickly enough?" Lucas asked.

Gramps hated it when you were late exploiting an opening

the defense had presented to you. *He who hesitates*, Gramps liked to say, *loses an easy bucket.*

"Can't even remember the ball touching your hands," Gramps said.

Lucas ran and collected the ball so Gramps didn't have to, dribbled back to the top of the key himself, giving his grandfather a low-five as he passed him.

"Let's do it again," Gramps said.

This time Gramps held the ball high over his head and told Lucas to make a sharp cut so close he could brush hips with Gramps on the way by. Lucas did that, streaking for the basket down the right side of the lane. Out of the corner of his eye, he saw his grandfather turn, pivot to his right, and then hit Lucas with a perfect chest pass before Lucas laid the ball in.

"All night long," Sam Winston said.

Fine with me, Lucas thought.

The night air was starting to get much colder. Lucas barely noticed. By now he'd worked up a good sweat. He was as into the drills they were running as if this were an official practice, and his teammates were out here with him.

But it was better than that.

It was basketball and it was Gramps.

Lucas loved his mom, totally and completely. He knew how difficult it had been for her without a partner, trying to be two parents at once. He knew how hard she had tried to tell him about his father, trying to tell the story of his life through old photographs and old home videos. Gramps had done the same. Lucas understood they were trying to explain the person and the father he'd lost. He could see how much they both had loved his dad. He sometimes imagined how awesome it would have been to have both his parents and his grandfather around.

But as hard as he tried, he couldn't feel a sense of loss about someone—and something—he'd never had.

It was why he loved Gramps as much as he did. Lucas knew he was trying to be grandfather and father the way his mom was trying to be father and mother to Lucas. And that was all right. Sometimes he would get sad when he'd look at the pictures of his dad holding him when he was a baby. Or looking at a video of his dad holding him on his first Christmas.

But he was still happier with what he had than sad about what he'd never had. He'd read one time that sometimes you didn't have to go looking for heroes, because they found you. He had his mom. He had his grandfather. He had a lot.

When they were finished working on the pick-and-roll, Gramps kept feeding Lucas the ball so he could work on his outside shot, which was getting better all the time. Even at the age of twelve, Lucas knew he was a pass-first point guard. He liked making a great pass more than a good shot. But as many assists as he'd gotten last season, and Gramps swore Lucas had led the league, and even though he'd been named to the Twin Lakes All-Star Team, he could see guys playing off him, daring him to shoot from the outside, making it harder for him to drive to the basket, and create opportunities for himself and the Wolves when he did.

He had vowed that this season would be different.

His free throws were still the worst part of his game, the one area where he wasn't confident, where his nerves would often get the best of him. Lucas loved being in motion, whether he had the ball or not. Then he'd get to the line and be standing still, and it was like he felt frozen. But Gramps told him that the more confident he got with his outside shot, the more that would translate to his free throws. If you could do one, he said, you could do the other.

It *had* to get better, or he couldn't have the ball in his hands at the end of a close game. He would be worrying about getting fouled and going to the line and maybe having to decide the game there.

Tonight he felt good from the line, hot on the cold night, making eight of his last ten.

But they weren't quite finished.

"Okay," Gramps said. "Down one. You just got fouled trying

to make a layup. Ended up on your butt. Two shots to win the game."

Lucas took the ball, stepped to the line, and went through the new pre-shot routine they were trying this season: ball on his left hip to start. Three dribbles, looking at the basket the whole time. Breathe in, breathe out. Bend the knees. Let it go.

Swish.

"Tie game," Gramps said, grabbing the ball after it went through the net. He bounce-passed it back to Lucas, smiling the Santa Claus smile again. "Did I mention that it's the championship game and there's only one second showing on the clock?"

Lucas smiled back.

"I felt as if that was one of your implied-type things," he said.

Put the ball on his hip. Three dribbles. Breathe. Bend. Shoot.

Swish.

Gramps came over and put his arm around him.

"Ball don't lie," he said.

Others in Lucas Winston's life would lie before the season was over. He just didn't know that at Westley Park. Not yet.

TWO

Lucas invited Gramps in for homemade apple pie left over from dinner when they pulled up in front of the house on Cypress Lane. It was the only house Lucas had ever known.

"Doc says I have to cut down on the sweets," Gramps said. "More old man stuff."

"You keep talking about how old you are," Lucas said. "But we were talking after practice the other day, and we all wish we had as much energy as you do."

"All I can do now is talk a good game," he said.

His grandfather leaned over from behind the wheel, kissed

Lucas on the cheek, and told him he'd see him tomorrow night at practice.

Lucas asked what he was going to do when he got home.

"Watch a game," he said.

"Which one?"

"Any one," Gramps said.

The car didn't pull away until Lucas was inside the front door and waving out at his grandfather. Lucas's mom was at the kitchen table, grading papers. She taught English at the small college in town, St. Luke's.

She looked at Lucas over her reading glasses and smiled.

"I was thinking after you left tonight," Julia Winston said, "that if I added up your official practices with the Wolves and your unofficial practices with your grandfather, basketball is as much of a job for you as seventh grade is."

"But I don't think of it as a job, Mom," Lucas said. "A job is cleaning my room."

"I'm glad you brought that up," she said, still smiling at him.

"I should have known I was walking into a trap," he said. "But I promise I'll do it at halftime of the game."

"There's always a game," she said.

"It's the Celtics," he said.

If LeBron was Lucas's favorite player, the Celtics were his favorite team, because they had been his dad's team. Same with his mom. And they shared the same favorite Celtic, Jayson Tatum, the small foward from Duke whom Lucas was sure was going to be one of the best players in the league someday, probably soon.

"I've got a better idea," she said. "Why don't you run upstairs and clean your room now, and then maybe we'll have a conversation about you maybe being able to watch till the end of the game tonight."

"Who's the best mom in the world?" he said.

"The one who will only consider letting you stay up late if your room passes inspection," she said. "Which would be the same mom who plans on watching some of the game with you as soon as I finish reading these papers."

It wasn't that she didn't like basketball. She did. She had told Lucas plenty of times about how much she'd loved watching his dad play when he was the star at Claremont High School, at least before he tore up his knee his senior year, doing enough damage to it that he lost out on any chance at a college scholarship. Gramps had talked more about the player Michael Winston had been, the kind of star high school point guard he wanted Lucas to grow up to be.

But instead of playing in college, he'd become a pre-med student. After college he went to med school, and a few years after graduating from med school he became the youngest team doctor in the history of the Boston Celtics, an orthopedic surgeon specializing in the kind of ACL tear that had ended his career.

He was only in his early thirties. If he couldn't still play basketball himself, he was working for the team that had been *his* team growing up. Then he had gotten sick. Lucas had read up on the kind of pancreatic cancer that had taken his dad from him before he even knew him. The only blessing, according to Gramps and his mom, was that it had happened fast. According to them, he had been diagnosed at Thanksgiving, and died a couple months after the one and only Christmas he had been able to share with his baby son. Now Lucas was only able to have Christmases with his dad in the pictures, and the videos.

"You can't live your life fixed on what you never had," Gramps had said to Lucas more than once. "You start doing that, it will eat away at your heart."

Then he'd say to Lucas, "The key to real happiness in this world is appreciating what you have, and knowing what you want. Everything else is just noise."

Lucas wasn't sure what the noise part meant. But he trusted that his grandfather knew what he was talking about, and not just because he'd lived as long as he had. He trusted him to know what was right, and not just on a basketball court.

Some nights Gramps would come over and watch a game

with Lucas on television. Some nights his mom would watch with Lucas, and they'd turn off the sound on the television, and each of them would read a book. Lucas figured he'd probably been born with a love of basketball in him, because of both his dad and Gramps. But he knew he'd gotten his love of reading from his mom.

But she remained a basketball fan herself. A couple times a year, she'd manage to score tickets to a Celtics game, and she and Gramps and Lucas would make the two-hour car ride to Boston, usually on a Friday or Saturday night. It was just one of about a thousand ways Lucas's mom could find to show him how much she loved him. And she never missed one of *his* games.

"You're sure you're not too tired to watch?" Lucas said after he had cleaned up his room. The game was still in the first quarter.

"Tired of us losing to the Pistons right now," she said.

"It's the end of a long road trip," Lucas said.

"We still can't be losing to the Pistons," she said.

He'd finished his homework before he'd left for Westley Park. He'd done a really good job on his room, not even tossing any clothes under the bed, as much of a hurry as he was in. Now he was next to his mom on the couch. As usual, Lucas had his laptop out so he could follow what was happening in other games around the NBA. For now, though, he was focused on the Celtics, who seemed to be making up a ten-point deficit in a blink, mostly because of the defense and ballhandling and passing of Jayson Tatum, who was suddenly on a rip. Tatum had just driven down the lane and then kicked out a no-look pass to Gordon Hayward in the corner. Then Hayward drained a wide-open three-pointer.

"Gramps says that people always talk about the open man in basketball," Lucas said to his mom. "But he says they should talk about the *most* open man."

"He used to say the same thing to your dad," she said, and sighed so loudly it made both of them laugh. "All the time."

On the screen, Tatum made another steal, drove the ball down the court with Hayward, the taller guy, on his left. Two-on-one fast break. But this time Tatum gave the defender a head fake, the defender moved over in front of Hayward, and Tatum drove past him, and elevated and dunked the ball.

When the first quarter ended, the score was tied. His mom said there was something to do in the kitchen. She came back about five minutes later with the popcorn she'd just heated in the microwave.

"Who's the best mom in the world?" Lucas said again.

"I believe that question has already been asked and answered," she said.

Then she said, "How's Gramps?"

"I hate it when he talks so much about being old," Lucas said.

"He *is* old, honey," she said.

"I just don't want him going anywhere," Lucas said.

"Your grandfather," she said, "is healthy as a horse. And you know why? Because of all the good he has in him."

"I just don't want anything to happen to him," Lucas said.

His mom reached for the remote and muted the game. "Where's this coming from?"

"He just seems to talk more and more about being an old man," Lucas said. "He even used that as an excuse for not coming in for apple pie and ice cream."

"He's just watching what he eats so he stays around for a long time," Julia said. "And you know that joking about his age is kind of his thing."

She leaned over now and pulled Lucas close to her.

"He *is* going to be around for a long, long time," she said. "And would you like to know the reason why?"

"Why?"

"You."

THREE

I t was the last practice before the Wolves' first game, in the gym at Claremont Middle, at seven o'clock on Thursday night.

Gramps was running the practice, as usual, but getting plenty of help from his assistant coach, who happened to be Ryan Moretti's mom. Mrs. Moretti had played college ball at the University of Connecticut, and her team had won two national championships while she was there. She had been the kind of point guard Lucas wanted to be: could shoot a basketball nearly as well as she could pass one.

One time Lucas and Ryan had looked at a highlight film of Mrs. Moretti somebody had put together on YouTube. When it was over Lucas had looked at his best friend and said, "I'm just gonna say it."

"Say what?" Ryan said.

Lucas said, "I want to play like a girl."

Tonight they walked through a couple new plays that Gramps had drawn up for them, and kept walking through them until Gramps felt the players had them down. Then he said what they had been waiting to hear from the time they had shown up at the gym:

"Let's go full court."

As much as he loved teaching, Gramps said that competition taught players more than he ever could. It's why he never called them scrimmages. He called them practice games. The first night of practice, he'd told them all ten players were good enough to start. He also told them that he wasn't nearly as interested in the players starting games as he was in the ones finishing them.

"Those are the minutes you boys ought to be trying to earn, every single game," Gramps said.

But his starters, at least to open the season, were Lucas and Ryan, Billy Goldman at center, Sharif Mustafa at shooting guard, and Richard Dichard at power forward. Even as deep as their bench was, and as talented as the other five players were, Lucas honestly felt that their starting five was better than any team in the Twin Lakes League.

But it didn't matter how good they thought they were. They had to go out and prove it, starting with their opener against Homestead. They had to do what players on good teams always did: bring out the best in one another. It was why you played the season. It was why Lucas waited the rest of the year for the season to begin. It was why he felt the best part of his school year—or whole year—was about to begin.

Some of the things he loved about basketball also applied to his other sports, spacing and smart ball movement and imagination. Especially imagination. Even when Lucas was running Gramps's plays, there was still room for him to be creative. To use his imagination. There were always decisions to make. There were always options. You just had to pick the best one.

At the same time you had the chance to do something just as much fun: try to think one move ahead of the other guys.

Or two.

"Some players can take a picture of where everybody is on the court at a given moment," Gramps said. "But the gift you have is that you can see where everybody is *about* to be, once you make your move."

That's the way it happened tonight, at the end of their

practice game, the two sides tied. Lucas had the ball after a made basket. Matt Sample was guarding him. Bobby Clapper was guarding Ryan.

Lucas yelled out, "Utah!"

He saw Ryan smile as he did, from the low blocks on the left side. "Utah" meant they were going to run a classic pick-and-roll that the Jazz used to run when they had John Stockton and Karl Malone. Both of them had ended up in the Hall of Fame, Lucas knew.

The pick-and-roll helped get them there. Mightily.

Now Lucas and Ryan were going to run it at Claremont Middle, with every player on the court knowing what was coming.

Let them try to stop it, Lucas thought.

Now he felt himself smiling.

The play had been effective for the starters the last two times they had used it. Both times Lucas had been the finisher. One time Matt had fought through Ryan's screen, but Lucas had still beaten him off the dribble and ended up with a layup. The other time Bobby Clapper had switched out on him, but not quickly enough, because Lucas had enough time and enough room to step back and make his longest shot of the night.

The other three starters, Billy and Richard and Sharif, were on the right side of the court. The key, both Lucas and Ryan knew, was that Ryan couldn't rush the action and pop out too soon. When he did come running at Lucas, Bobby Clapper yelled "screen," the way they'd been taught. Matt would come up now on Lucas and guard him closer than he already was.

Lucas was sure it wasn't going to matter.

He'd stepped back to his left last time. The time before that he'd driven right. Matt guessed Lucas was going right again, because right meant a layup. Lucas took one dribble to his right, then crossed over, as if about to use his great first step and drive.

From behind Ryan, Bobby Clapper could see that Lucas had a step on Matt, and a clear path down the lane unless somebody jumped out on him from the other side of the defense.

That's what the picture looked like right now.

Lucas had a different idea about the way he wanted the court to look next. And if Ryan was reading his mind the way he so often could, so did he.

As soon as Ryan had set the pick on Matt, he was gone, reverse-pivoting, on his way back to the low blocks on the left. Instead of driving, Lucas pulled up at the free-throw line, went into his shooting motion as if about to take a jump shot. Travis Brady was in front of Lucas in the lane now, long arms in the air.

They just weren't long enough.

Lucas elevated as much as he could, which wasn't a whole lot, and without even looking, passed the ball to Ryan. Ryan caught the ball with the softest hands on the team, chest high, and seemed to shoot it all in one motion. Easy layup, off the backboard, through the net. Practice game over. Ryan came over and gave Lucas a quick high five. They went to get water. If a practice game like this hadn't gotten them ready for the season, nothing would.

Gramps came over, sat next to Lucas on the bottom row of the bleachers, and put his arm around him.

"I know how hard you work at this, son," he said. "But I know you've got a gift for this game too. And you've got to make sure you always honor it."

"I will," Lucas said.

The old man pulled him closer.

"Promise me," he said, his voice suddenly husky.

"Promise," Lucas said.

"If you don't," Gramps said, "you'll regret it for the rest of your life."

Lucas looked up at him. For a moment he thought his tough old grandfather might cry. That was the thing about Gramps, he thought. He could always surprise you, sometimes when you least expected it.

FOUR

Lucas wasn't a huge fan of all his seventh-grade classes. He loved reading and writing, though. which is the reason Mr. Collins's English class was his favorite. Nothing else was even close.

Mr. Collins had told them on the first day of class in September that the first rule of being a good writer was being a good reader. And in his conferences with Lucas, he constantly reminded him that being a good writer was a lot like being a good basketball player, or a good athlete in any sport:

The harder you worked at it, the better you got.

It was why, at one of their after-school conferences, Mr. Collins suggested that Lucas start keeping a journal.

"Like one of those 'Dear Diary' things?" Lucas said. "No way."

Mr. Collins grinned.

"It won't be like that," he said, "not if you do it right. The object is to write something every day about something that happened to you, even if it's only a couple of paragraphs. Think of it as telling your life story, just a little bit at a time. If you want to write about what happened with your basketball team, write about that. Again, it doesn't have to be long. I can see already this will be a good exercise for you. Someday, when you're as old as me, you won't believe how lucky you'll feel that you can go back and see what was happening to you when you were twelve."

"You mean like looking at an old picture?" Lucas said.

He thought of the photographs of his dad, and wished they came with a story.

"It will be way better than that," Mr. Collins said. "It shouldn't feel like a job. You could try to do it every day, but it's not like the stars will fall out of the heavens if you miss a day. The big thing is to keep the story going."

Lucas started writing about basketball after the Wolves' first practice, showing the journal to Mr. Collins every few days.

He was already getting a sense of what was his best work and what wasn't. Mostly what he got from Mr. Collins, who was a basketball fan himself, was encouragement. The work, he said, was paying off. Lucas was a better writer by November than he'd been when the school year started.

It was also way more fun than Lucas thought it was going to be. The first few days were a bit of a grind, trying to decide what was worth writing about. After a while, though, it started to click. Sometimes he'd write everything down as soon as he got home, as a way of making sure not to forget the things he *did* want to write about that day. Sometimes he'd have to wait until after he did his real homework. He made sure to never let the journal get in the way of his other schoolwork. Lucas prided himself on getting good grades, even in the classes he didn't love as much as English. Sometimes he'd even miss some of a basketball game he was planning to watch on television because he wanted to get upstairs and write. He didn't want to miss a day.

Sometimes he'd describe a good play he'd made, like the pass to Ryan to end the practice game. Sometimes he'd write down one of Gramps's sayings, or some story Mrs. Moretti had told about her career, since Gramps never talked very much about his own.

When Lucas would try to get something out of him, Gramps would always say pretty much the same thing.

"One thing I do to at least *try* to keep myself young," he said, "is to not be one of those old goats living in the past."

"But you love basketball history," Lucas said.

"Always remember something," Gramps said. "The past is a nice place to visit sometimes. You just don't want to stay there."

That one went right into the journal.

In class that afternoon, Mr. Collins said it was time for a new writing assignment. The last one had been about friendship, and why friendship mattered. Lucas hadn't just written about Ryan, but about Maria Chen, his other best friend.

"This is going to be a fun one," Mr. Collins said.

"They're always fun," Maria said.

From the desk behind Maria, Ryan said, "Speak for yourself."

"C'mon, Ryan," Mr. Collins said. "We both know what kind of writer you can be when you apply yourself."

"It's not the writing I mind," Ryan said. "It's the *rewriting.*"

"But good writing *is* rewriting," Mr. Collins said.

Ryan put his head down on his desk, as if that were the saddest thing he'd ever heard.

"I know," he said. "I *know.*"

The rest of his classmates laughed. Even Ryan was laughing when he picked his head up.

"So what is the new topic?" Maria said.

"I want you all to write a short biography," Mr. Collins said. "You all know what a biography is, right?"

Lucas raised his hand. The journal he was keeping was more like his own autobiography, a day at a time, but he knew the difference between that and a biography.

"You tell the story of somebody else's life," Lucas said.

"Exactly," Mr. Collins said.

He was sitting on the front of his desk, legs dangling over the side. As usual he was wearing a pair of classic sneakers. These were old red-and-black Air Jordans, as cool as Mr. Collins was.

You could tell he loved teaching English the way Gramps loved teaching basketball.

"Who's the biography supposed to be about?" Maria said.

"Someone you admire," Mr. Collins said. "But here's a little twist: It can't be a parent."

Lucas smiled, because he'd already decided who his subject would be.

"Can it be someone who's *like* a parent?" he said.

Mr. Collins scratched his head, as if trying to look confused. "Gee," he said, "can anybody help me out with who Lucas might be talking about here?"

"Gramps," Ryan said.

"One hundred percent," Maria said.

"So can it?" Lucas said.

"Absolutely," Mr. Collins said. Then he told them that he was giving them more time to this assignment than he ever had before, that it wasn't due until right before their Christmas break next month.

Best assignment yet, Lucas thought. And already his favorite, even if he hadn't started.

He reached across the aisle and gave Ryan a low-five.

"This is going to be like a layup for you," Ryan Moretti said.

Little did they know.

FIVE

Gramps drove Lucas and Ryan to Claremont Middle for the Homestead game, which was scheduled for eleven o'clock on Saturday morning.

"Nothing better than Opening Day," Gramps said when they were inside. "Always feels like New Year's to me."

They were the first ones to the gym.

Gramps was underneath the basket, feeding balls to Lucas and Ryan. Gramps even wanted layups shot the right way. He wanted everything done the right way.

"Don't duck your head when you release the ball, Mr.

Moretti," Gramps said. "You pick a spot on the backboard and fix your eye on it like it's a bull's-eye."

"But Mr. Winston," Ryan said, "I never miss layups."

"And if you keep focusing on the fundamentals," Gramps said, "you never will."

Gramps fed him another bounce pass. Ryan caught it, then laid the ball in off the backboard. Head up.

"Gramps," Lucas said. "Sometimes I think you'd rather have fundamentals for breakfast instead of cereal."

The old man managed a smile that seemed to fight its way through his game face.

The rest of the Wolves began to arrive. The six rows of bleachers began to fill up with parents and grandparents and brothers and sisters of the players. Lucas saw Maria up there too. Her brother, Neil, was the backup shooting guard, and sometimes replaced Ryan at small forward.

Lucas's mom showed up about ten minutes before they were ready to start. She'd always told Lucas she was more of a game mom than a warm-up mom.

"I never miss the good parts," she told Lucas.

"And what parts are those?" he said.

"They generally start when the ref hands you the ball," she said.

Lucas was even more excited than normal today because

not only was the Twin Lakes season about to begin, it was beginning with a rivalry game. Claremont and Homestead were neighboring towns. It only took about ten minutes, by car, to get from downtown Claremont to downtown Homestead, and so it didn't matter what the sport was, at what age level. When it was Claremont vs. Homestead it was like the Yankees playing the Red Sox in baseball, or Duke playing North Carolina in basketball, or Ohio State and Michigan in college football.

First game of the season, or championship game at the end, Claremont vs. Homestead was always a very big deal. And there was another reason why Lucas always loved playing against the Homestead Bulls: Charlie Patten. He wasn't just a good point guard. Charlie was a great one, even though he was probably the smallest player in the league this season. It always looked like a mismatch, size-wise, when Lucas and Charlie stood next to each other, as if Charlie had gotten caught in a switch. But once the game started it wasn't a mismatch at all, it was a totally fair fight, even when it was just pickup games in the summer at a park in Claremont, or one in Homestead. Charlie Patten was such a wizard with the ball, so fast and so tricky, that sometimes Lucas called him Harry Potter.

The two of them shook hands at mid court after both teams had finished their warm-ups.

"Here we go again," Lucas said to him.

They'd been playing against each other in travel ball since the fifth grade.

"We should be sick of each other by now," Charlie said.

He had a lot of red hair and even more freckles.

"But we're not," Lucas said.

"Probably all the way through high school," Charlie said.

"Fine by me," Lucas said.

Charlie grinned, then reached out and bumped Lucas some fist.

As small as Charlie was, the rest of his team was tall, and long. The Bulls' next best player, after Charlie, was the guy Ryan would be guarding, Darrell Zimmer. Zim was built more like a tight end than a small forward. And he was fast. He could handle the ball outside if he had to, and was a bear underneath the basket. Ryan liked to say that when Zim had you boxed out, you felt as if you had to run around a city block trying to get a rebound. But Ryan loved the challenge of going up against him the way Lucas welcomed the challenge of going up against Charlie.

Gramps gathered the Wolves around him, right in front of their bench. As much as his grandfather could talk your ear off about basketball if you let him, he always kept his comments brief once there was a game about to break out. He liked to say that if he'd done a good enough job in practice, once they did get to game day, basketball would be exactly what it was supposed to be: the players' game.

"Run when you can," Gramps said. "Run our stuff in the half-court when we have to set up. And you all know what we're going to do on defense."

"See the ball," Lucas said.

Sam Winston smiled then, as happy to be in this gym as they were.

"Where else," he said to the Wolves, "would any of us rather be right now?"

Where the Wolves didn't want to be, as things turned out, was down ten points to the Bulls by the end of the first quarter.

They were doing what Gramps had told them to do, fast-breaking when they could. They were running their basic sets in the half-court. That wasn't the problem. The problem was that they weren't making any shots, and the Bulls were making theirs. Simple as that.

It was like the announcers always said on TV: Basketball was a miss-make sport. And the Wolves were missing all over the place.

"We're fine," Gramps said when they were back at the bench after the quarter. "Our shots will start to fall. But until they do, let's press those guys all over the court."

He subbed in Neil for Sharif, and Liam O'Rourke for Richard. The Wolves got a little smaller in the process, but also got a lot more tenacious on defense. Gramps told Neil and Liam to double-team the ball every chance they got. And he told them to cover for Lucas when he took some chances and went for steals, even in the backcourt.

The press worked right away. The Wolves were the ones playing faster now, and more aggressively. Lucas did make a couple quick steals. The Wolves began the second quarter with an 8–0 run, and just like that, they were within a basket. When Lucas made another steal and fed Ryan for an easy basket, the game was tied.

Lucas gave a quick look over to the bench. Gramps just sat there with his arms crossed in front of him, looking the same way he had when they were falling behind. But the press had changed everything. The Wolves' not-so-secret weapon had already made his presence felt, in the first half of the first game of the season.

The game was still tied at halftime. It was still tied at the end of the third quarter. Gramps had done plenty of substituting by then, experimenting with different combinations, as if letting the Wolves decide which five would be on the court at the end today.

But with two minutes left and the Wolves up by a basket,

he called a time-out and put his five starters back into the game.

He looked down at the scoreboard, then back at the players sitting in front of him.

"Since the game *does* count," he said, "and since the other team *is* Homestead, I can't think of a single reason why we shouldn't haul off and win this thing."

As Lucas started to walk back on the court with his teammates, Gramps gave a quick tug on his arm.

"That big kid guarding Ryan is gassed," Gramps said.

He meant Zim.

"Make him defend the pick-and-roll every single time you can," Gramps said.

"Got it," Lucas said.

Lucas started to pull away. Gramps still had his arm. But he was grinning.

"If he *can* defend that thing," he said.

The Wolves had the ball in the backcourt. Lucas brought it up. Charlie darted in a couple times, going for the steal. Lucas was ready for him. Lucas didn't call out "Utah" as he crossed half-court. All he had to do was look at Ryan. They both knew.

Ryan knew. Zim knew. Charlie knew what was coming and so did Lucas.

Let them try to stop it.

　　　　　　　　　　　　　　　　　MIKE LUPICA

Lucas angled to the right side when he got to the top of the key. He was right-handed. Charlie knew Lucas was more comfortable driving right with his dominant hand. But now Lucas crossed over and went left toward the free-throw line.

Ryan was there by then. Zim was behind Ryan, and jumped out as Lucas cleared Ryan, seeing that Lucas had a step on Charlie. So now it was Zim guarding Lucas, Charlie on Ryan.

Charlie had time to get in front of Ryan as Ryan turned for the basket, guarding him as closely as he could, knowing what kind of height advantage Ryan would have down near the basket if Lucas passed him the ball.

But Lucas caught Ryan's eye. As he did, he tilted his head slightly to his right, telling Ryan to pop out behind the same three-point line they used in their league that players used in high school. He was telling Ryan to go for what the TV guys called the "dagger."

Charlie, fast as he was, was slow to react when Ryan didn't make a move for the basket, and ran out to the line instead. Lucas didn't hesitate. He wheeled and hit Ryan with a chest-high pass. Ryan didn't even need a dribble. He just put a pure shooting stroke on his shot, even holding his follow-through just slightly.

All net.

Now the Wolves were up by five, 39–34.

The Bulls came back and scored. But then Billy made a baby hook, his favorite shot. The Wolves were back up by five. Twenty seconds left. The Bulls tried to run a pick-and-roll of their own at the other end with Charlie and Zim, but Ryan fought through Zim's screen, got a hand on the ball, slapped it over to Lucas, who beat everybody down the court. Only Lucas didn't shoot the ball. They were under ten seconds now, and instead of driving all the way to the basket, he cut to the corner while Charlie chased him, then back toward half-court until the buzzer sounded, ending the game.

Sometimes when you were the open man, all you had to do was dribble out the clock.

They were 1–0.

SIX

ramps treated the players to a pizza lunch in town at Gus's. The Wolves took up two long tables in the back room.

While Lucas and Ryan waited for their pizzas to come out of the kitchen, Lucas told his friend it felt as if they were celebrating a championship, and not just the first game of the season.

"Fine by me," Ryan said. "Sometimes I think it's okay to celebrate the beginning of something the way you do the ending."

"I thought you were just thinking about your first slice," Lucas said.

"That too," Ryan said. "Like you're not?"

"What I've been thinking about is the way you waited until the exact right moment to pop out for that three-pointer," Lucas said.

"You know I saw you give me the nod," he said.

"And I knew you knew," Lucas said.

"Gotta admit, though, the play was pretty chill," Ryan said. "But if you really think about it, I was only open that much because of you."

"How do you figure?"

"Zim decided he wasn't going to let you beat them with a drive," Ryan said. "So he overplayed right away. And then you beat them with the dish."

"It doesn't matter if you don't make the shot," Lucas said. "Plus, you're a better shooter than I am."

"In today's game maybe," Ryan said.

"Only game that matters right now," Lucas said.

Lucas's mom and Ryan's mom were at a table against the wall. Lucas heard his mom say, "Is there anything better than watching hungry boys eat pizza?"

"But aren't they always hungry?" Ryan's mom said.

"Even when they're sleeping, pretty sure."

Gramps wasn't sitting with Lucas and Ryan. He was at the head of the other table, his slice of plain pizza untouched in front of him. He was hunched over his napkin, smiling as he scribbled on it.

Ryan followed Lucas's eyes over to where Gramps sat.

"What's he doing?" Ryan said.

"I'll bet you my allowance and yours that he's diagramming a new play because of something that happened in the game today," Lucas said.

"Not taking that bet," Ryan said.

"Chicken?"

"We both know you're right," Ryan said. "I'm surprised that *X*s and *O*s don't come spilling out of his ear sometimes."

Lucas grinned. "I think his hearing aid keeps them trapped inside," he said.

Everything felt right today. They hadn't just won their opener, they'd won a rivalry game. They'd beaten a team they knew they might face for the championship—again—if the season went the way they thought it would go, and hoped it would go. Had they played their best game? No one expected that in their first game. They sure hadn't looked like much of a championship team in the first quarter. But they had fought their way out of that ten-point hole. Sometimes what mattered most in sports was overcoming something. It brought out the best in you.

When the game had ended Gramps had said, "Anybody can

get knocked down. Heck, I used to do it all the time. There's no trick in that. Any old crumbum can do that."

It was one of his favorite words: crumbum.

"It's how you get yourself back up after you do get knocked down, or even knocked back, that tells you plenty about yourself. And the other team, too."

Lucas knew that Gramps's wife—his grandmom—had died in a nursing home when Lucas was just two years old. But Gramps said he'd lost her years before that, and that by the time she finally passed, all her memories were gone. Just not his. He still called her his "best girl."

Now he lived in an apartment within walking distance of Lucas and his mom's house on Cypress. And while he didn't have dinner with them every night, he had dinner with them most nights. Lucas's mom said that the table just didn't look right to her when it was set for two, instead of three. Julia's own parents had moved to Oregon, on the other side of the country and what felt like the other side of the world, because her dad's only brother lived out there. Lucas and his mom now visited them every other year. His other granddad would make sure that when they did come visit, he would get tickets to a Trailblazers' game. His other grandfather was a basketball fan too. Just not the way Gramps was.

After Gus's, Lucas and Ryan went back to Ryan's house and

watched college basketball, Georgetown against Villanova. But as soon as it was halftime Lucas suggested they go out in Ryan's driveway and play a game of H-O-R-S-E.

"But it's cold out there," Ryan said. "And nice and toasty in here. And I'm just throwing this out there, but didn't we just have a game?"

"Now we can have another game, just the two of us," Lucas said. "You know you want to. You love playing H-O-R-S-E against me. Like I said, you're a better shooter than I am."

"Okay," Ryan said, grinning. "I can't argue with you on that."

"Come on, it'll be a blast," Lucas said. "We can start getting ready for next Saturday's game."

It was a road game, against Essex.

"You look tired to me," Ryan said, even though he knew he would end up losing this fight in the end. "You should rest."

"After we play H-O-R-S-E," Lucas said.

"Don't you ever get tired of basketball?" Ryan said.

"Don't *you* ever get tired of asking me that question?" Lucas said. "Because the answer is the same every single time."

Ryan sighed loudly, got up off the couch, and headed up the stairs. Lucas already had his jacket back on.

"One game," Ryan said.

"Promise," Lucas said.

"And don't pull that thing where when I win you make me

stay out and keep playing until you can win," Ryan said.

"When have I ever done that?" Lucas said, grinning to himself.

"Always!" Ryan said. "You don't even want to stop playing when it's dark out."

There was still a lot of sun when they got outside, even though it would be December soon. But the day had gotten a lot colder since they'd left Gus's, so they did some running around before they started, just to get themselves as warm as possible.

Lucas let Ryan shoot first. He used to just stand outside and fire away, because his outside shot really was more pure than Lucas's. Just not anymore. Lucas hadn't only been working on his outside shot at practice, and with Gramps at the park, he'd been doing it on his own driveway basket. He knew that the more dangerous he became with his outside shot, the more dangerous he became as a point guard. If the guy guarding him was afraid to give him space, it made it easier for Lucas to drive past him and create a shot for himself or one of his teammates.

Ryan got ahead early. Lucas came back with a couple left-handed floaters, which he knew always annoyed Ryan, because being better with his left hand, his off hand, was about the only edge he had out here.

But when they were finally tied at H-O-R-S, it was Lucas

who stepped back all the way to Ryan's mailbox, and buried two straight shots. Ryan matched the first, but not the second. Because it was game point, he got one last chance.

He missed again.

Ryan said, "I don't like to make excuses when I occasionally do lose to you."

"That would be so unlike you," Lucas said.

"But I think my shooting arm was tired after I made that absolute bomb at the end against the Bulls," Ryan said.

"Well, now you can rest it," Lucas said, "because of those two absolute bombs I just made."

By the time Lucas walked up the street from Ryan's house to his own, Gramps was waiting for him. It meant he was waiting to talk about the game they'd won. If practice was his favorite thing about coaching, breaking down a game after it had been played was his next favorite.

Then came actually coaching the game.

Lucas pointed that out to him while they ate turkey meatloaf and mashed potatoes and green beans.

"That press changed everything today," Lucas said.

"Even I picked up on that," Julia said. "The poor boys on the other team looked as if they'd been attacked by a swarm of bees."

Gramps smiled. "Well, maybe that decision did tilt the game slightly toward us at that point," he said.

"You *think?*" his grandson said.

Gramps picked up his water glass. As always, Lucas couldn't believe how big his hands were, and how long his fingers were. They were old hands, and there were a lot of dark spots on them. But these were great, big basketball hands. When the old man was feeling frisky, he would palm a ball with one hand after he got one spinning on the index finger of the other.

"You boys still had to execute the press properly," Gramps said.

"Yeah," Lucas said, smiling. "I heard somewhere it's a player's game."

"Well, it sure as heck isn't a coach's game," Gramps said, "even though there's a whole lot of coaches who act as if they invented basketball, instead of just putting their players in the best position to win the game."

"Which is what you did today," Lucas said.

"Eat your beans," his grandfather said, "even though you're pretty much full of beans already."

"Wonder who he gets *that* from?" Lucas's mom said.

"Must be your side of the family," Gramps said.

After Lucas had finished his apple pie, he said to Gramps, "Hey, we've been talking so much about the game I forgot to tell you guys about this cool writing project Mr. Collins gave us in English."

He explained it, and how it couldn't be a parent.

"Good!" Lucas's mom said, sounding so relieved that she wasn't going to be his subject that they all laughed.

Then she said, "Even though I sort of know what the answer to this question is going to be, gonna ask it anyway: Whose life story are you going to write?"

"Gramps," Lucas said.

"Oh, come on," Gramps said. "Can't you find somebody more interesting than an old man?"

"First of all, you're not old," Lucas said.

Gramps turned to Lucas's mom.

"When was the last time the boy's eyes were checked?" he said.

"I want to write about you," Lucas said. "I want to know more about your life. There's got to be stuff you never told me."

"I can't even remember the things I *want* to remember," Gramps said.

"C'mon," Lucas said. "It'll be a blast."

He felt the way he did trying to persuade Ryan to go outside for a game of H-O-R-S-E.

Gramps smiled at Lucas now, and reached across the table with one of his old hands and squeezed Lucas's shoulder.

"You know me as well as you need to know me," he said, "even if I'm not as great as you think I am."

"How do you know, Gramps?" Lucas said.

Gramps smiled and said, "Because nobody could be."

He squeezed Lucas's shoulder again, got up from the table, and limped out of the room.

"Let's go watch some basketball," he said.

They were always on safe ground, Lucas knew, with basketball.

SEVEN

Lucas looked at his mom. She put out her hands and shrugged.

"I thought he'd be happy," Lucas said.

"Maybe it's the memory thing," she said. "You know he gets frustrated when he can't remember things, and even embarrassed."

"I know I could probably come up with another subject," Lucas said. "But he's the subject I want."

"The older you get," she said, "the more set you get in your ways." She lowered her voice. "Go easy with this tonight. He seems more tired than usual. Maybe that comeback took more out of him than you."

Gramps was at one end of the couch in the living room. There was a game on the television set. Lucas plopped down at the other end.

"What are you watching there?" Lucas said.

"Michigan State against Syracuse," he said. "Curious to see how State attacks that Syracuse zone."

There was a time-out in the game, and a commercial appeared on the TV screen. Lucas's mom called out from the kitchen, saying she was making a cup of tea and asking if Gramps wanted some. He politely declined.

"You know, Gramps," Lucas said, "I didn't mean to spring the idea of my paper on you. But I really think it will be fun."

Gramps sighed.

"You know what's another sign of knowing you're really old?" he said. "Talking about old *times* more and more. I see it with my friends. I sometimes get the idea that they think the best things that will ever happen to them have already happened."

"But you're never like that," Lucas said. "I just want to know more about stuff that happened to you."

Gramps turned now. He smiled, but looked tired.

"Find a player you admire instead," he said.

"But it won't be somebody I admire as much as I do you," Lucas said.

"I appreciate that," he said. "But you know what else I appreciate with young people like you, son, especially when they look at sports? That you think the good old days are now. So learn up on LeBron, or Steph, or Kawhi. I'd help you with a paper like that, and maybe learn a few things about history myself."

"But we could work on one about you together," Lucas said. "You always say that history makes you understand the present better, and not just basketball history."

"You understand me just fine already," Gramps said.

He reached for the remote next to him. The game was back on. Gramps muted it.

"I'm a lot more interested in what you're going to do next than in what I already did," Gramps said. "You want to know who really keeps me going? You do. You're the only one who can make me feel young, the way you and your teammates did in that game we played today."

"Maybe if I do this paper, it will jog your memory on some cool things," Lucas said.

"These knees of mine made me give up jogging a long time ago," Gramps said.

"Mom says that I never give up," Lucas said.

"Make an exception for me," Gramps said. "It's too late for me to get comfortable talking about myself. It's another thing people my age do. They talk too much, and live too little."

He stood up now. When he'd been seated for more than a few minutes, it took some effort. Sometimes it would even take him a couple tries to get off a couch or out of a chair. But he never asked for help, and didn't now.

"I'll see you at practice on Monday," he said to Lucas. Then he raised his voice slightly and said, "Thanks for dinner, Julia."

Lucas walked his grandfather to the front door. But as he opened it for him, Gramps suddenly pulled him into a bear hug.

"You had yourself a great day today," he said to Lucas. "What you should be focusing on is that."

"*We* had a great day," Lucas said.

"Have it your way," Gramps said. "Because all we've got is today."

He pulled out of the hug and stared at Lucas, and then looked down at him.

"Love you," Gramps said.

"Love you more," Lucas said.

Gramps smiled.

"No," he said, "you don't."

He closed the door. Lucas watched through the curtains of

the front window as he limped toward his car. As he did, he felt his mom's hand on his shoulder.

"I heard some of that," she said.

"Did it make sense to you?" Lucas said.

"He's a sweet, proud, shy, stubborn man," she said. "I always kid with him that he thinks people his own age are older than him. Maybe he really doesn't want to act like them."

"I'm kind of stubborn too," Lucas said.

"Wonder where you get it from?" his mom said.

"I want this to be a tribute to him," Lucas said. "I've just got to figure out a way to make him see that."

"Maybe he doesn't want a tribute," his mom said.

"Why not?" Lucas said.

"Because maybe he thinks it will sound like the kind of eulogy people give you when you're gone," she said.

EIGHT

On Monday in class, Mr. Collins said that the reason that he'd given them as long as he had to do the paper was because it was going to count for most of their first-semester grade.

"I'm challenging you all to do your very best work," he said. "But what I want you to do even more is challenge yourselves."

When he asked for a show of hands to find out how many of them had already picked their subject, Lucas only got his right hand up as high as his shoulder.

Mr. Collins saw, and smiled.

"Does that mean you've picked half a subject, Lucas?" he said.

"Having some trouble," he said.

"Picking a subject?"

"*With* my subject," he said.

"Can I help?"

Lucas said, "It's like the paper, I guess. I'll have to figure it out myself."

"I want the reporting on this to be as much fun as the writing," Mr. Collins said.

"Same," Lucas said.

Lucas wanted Gramps to change his mind on his own. But his mom was right. It was early in the game. Lucas wasn't giving up. That wasn't him. In anything.

On the way to the bus, Lucas asked Ryan if he'd picked his subject yet.

"No," he said. "I was glad that Mr. Collins was looking at you after he asked the question, because both my hands were on my desk."

"You'll come up with somebody good," Lucas said.

"It doesn't matter whether I do or not," Ryan said. "I'm no good at writing."

"You can write," Lucas said.

"Not like you."

"Nobody's asking you to write like me," he said. "You just have to write like you."

"You don't understand," Ryan said. "My dad told me last night that I've got to do better this semester than I did second semester last year. If I don't, I can't play sports second semester *this* year."

"What does 'better' mean?"

"No more *C*s," Ryan said.

"For real?"

"For real," he said. "Dad said he's not asking me to be an A student. But that he knows I'm capable of better work. My mom agrees with him. So if any of my grades tank, I won't be able to finish the season."

"So we won't let them tank," Lucas said.

"They're not your grades," Ryan said.

"We're a team, remember?"

"I can't write!" Ryan said.

"And I used to think I couldn't shoot from the outside," Lucas said.

"You practiced and got better," Ryan said.

"So can you."

"The difference is that you love basketball," Ryan said. "I'll *never* love English."

"Just think of the class," Lucas said, "as a game you refuse to lose. Or a match in tennis."

Ryan had gotten even better at tennis than he was at basketball over the last couple years, and was probably the best player their age in Claremont by now.

"I know I need a better attitude," Ryan said.

"I can help you with that, too," Lucas said.

"*A* for attitude?" Ryan said.

Ryan's mood had improved by practice that night. But then everybody's attitude seemed to improve once they were inside the gym at Claremont Middle. It wasn't just the sound of the gym, the bounce of the ball and the squeak of sneakers on the newly polished floor, and the swish of balls through the net, and even balls clanging off the rim. It was the sound of the chatter, too. Maria told Lucas how the music she played on the piano, or just the music she listened to, always made her feel better.

The sound of the gym was Lucas's music.

Lucas hadn't seen Gramps since Saturday night. Lucas didn't mention his paper. Neither did Gramps. It was all basketball tonight. They were back on familiar ground. Gramps just talked to the team about turning the page and getting ready for Saturday's away game against the Sheridan Sonics, before walking them through the new play he'd been diagramming on his napkin during the pizza party at Gus's.

Lucas knew that Gramps's plays always made perfect sense to him when he was drawing them up, on a napkin or piece of paper or even a newspaper. And when he'd finished drawing it up and began explaining it to Lucas, his eyes would light up and his hand would start going in all directions as he told Lucas that the point guard was supposed to go here and the screener there and what he thought the defense would do in response.

At first all the lines and arrows and *X*s and *O*s would make no sense to Lucas. But finally Gramps would look at him, eyes still bright, and say, *"See?"* as if the whole thing were as beautiful to him as a rainbow.

The new play tonight was a double high screen for Ryan and Billy. It didn't matter whether Lucas triggered the play from the right side of the court, or the left. Ryan would run up one side of the lane. Billy would run up the other. Then it would be up to Lucas where he would go with the ball. If he threw the ball to Ryan, Billy would immediately spin, then cut for the basket while Lucas was making his own cut, using Ryan as a screen.

Lucas would keep going to the basket, or pop out as Ryan turned with the ball, surveying the defense himself. He might end up with an open shot, or put the ball on the floor and head back for the basket himself. He might throw it to Billy. Or to Lucas.

What Gramps really wanted was to create as many distractions as possible for the defense.

"I call this one of our 'shiny object' plays," Gramps said.

"In this case, the ball is the shiny object. The other team worries so much about what the guy with it might do, they forget to watch for the open man. Or two open men, in this case."

There was that light in his eyes again. He was Gramps again. Maybe Lucas's mom had been right. Maybe everybody had a bad day, or night, once in a while. Lucas told himself that he still wasn't giving up on his paper, not by a long shot. He imagined that he was the one drawing up a great play, one that might just take a little extra time to develop. Then once he got started, once he started writing it, Gramps would see that all Lucas was doing was finding a new way to respect him, and even honor him.

Then the play would make sense to both of them.

But he wasn't going to bring it up tonight. They were having a good practice. They were coming off a good win. They had another game on Saturday, against a tough opponent. It was all ball tonight.

Gramps left enough time at the end for one of their practice games. He said they were going to do things a little differently tonight: All he was going to do was keep score, and run the clock. He made Lucas the coach of one team. He let Neil coach the other. As always, he didn't talk about the first unit or the second unit. He never did that, and was always telling Lucas he hated it when college and pro coaches used those expressions.

"The *team* is the unit," Gramps said. "You're either in, or you're out."

Each team could run as many or as few plays as it wanted. They could fast break as much, or as little, as they wanted. And press when they wanted. The starter wore blue mesh pinnies. The other guys wore red.

"Play like it's the playground tonight," he said. "But if somebody calls a foul, it sure as sugar better be a foul."

It was as if somebody had turned up the volume in the gym. The game was close. Every time Lucas or Ryan or Billy or Richard would get the blue team ahead by a couple baskets, the red team would come right back at them, riding the hot hand of Neil from the start.

They were finally a few minutes past when practice was supposed to have ended. The game was tied again. Gramps finally got up from the scorer's table where he'd been working the clock and said that since they couldn't play all night, he was going to flip a coin to determine which team would get the last possession.

Lucas got to call. He called heads.

Heads it was.

"Blues get one shot at this," Gramps said. "If they score, they win. If the reds get a stop, they win."

Lucas called his guys around him.

"Shiny object," he said.

Sharif inbounded the ball to Lucas at half-court. Lucas immediately cut all the way across the court to his left. Ryan and Billy came out from underneath the basket as he did. Ryan was closest to Lucas. Billy was over to Ryan's left.

Lucas still had his dribble. But now he crossed over, went to his right hand, and headed for Ryan. As soon as he did, Billy reverse-pivoted, headed down the right side of the lane, waving his right arm for the ball. Lucas passed it to Ryan. Ryan passed it right back. Lucas was at the free-throw line. Billy was down in the low blocks. Lucas was open. Billy was more open. Liam, who'd been guarding Ryan, was now guarding Lucas.

Lucas had enough space to shoot, even over Liam's long arms.

Just not enough.

Ryan cut down the left side of the lane, with a clear height advantage over Neil. Lucas eyeballed him the whole way. Then, at the last possible second, he turned and fired a perfect pass over the top of the defense to Billy.

Not the only open man.

Just the one who was most open.

Billy had squared himself up as the ball was in the air. All he had to do was catch and shoot, banking the ball softly off the backboard, then through the net. The sound the ball made was the last music of the night.

NINE

Gramps had been invited over for a late dinner after practice. He didn't really need the invitation. There was always a place for him at the table if he wanted it. But he said he was having a burger with his friend Ben, who'd just retired as the golf pro at Claremont's public golf course.

"But he's still giving a few lessons to some of his old students, just to keep a hand in," Gramps had told Lucas. "Once a teacher, always a teacher."

"You'll never stop teaching, either," Lucas said to him.

"One of these days," he said. "I just hope I don't have to be told when it's time for me to stop."

At dinner Lucas told his mom that he hadn't mentioned his writing assignment to Gramps tonight.

"Maybe next time you do, I can help," she said. "Soften him up a little, even though I know he's an old softie at heart. Maybe we can both make him see how important this is to you."

"I'm really kind of interested in what kind of player *he* was when he was young," Lucas said. "Did he ever tell you the name of the college he went to in California?" Lucas said. "Or did Dad?"

She made a helpless gesture with her hands.

"It never really came up that much," she said. "It's not like I spent a lot of time talking to your dad about *his* dad's basketball career. The few times the subject came up, Gramps would just say that it was a school that went out of business a long time ago."

"Did he finish college somewhere else?"

"I honestly don't know," Julia said.

"Dad must have known," Lucas said.

"It was just never a big topic of conversation with us," she said. "Your grandfather never really changes in this particular area. He only wants to focus on your career now. Back in the day, he only wanted to focus on your dad's, at least until your dad got hurt."

"Aren't you a little bit curious?" Lucas said.

His mom grinned. "Not as curious as you obviously are," she said.

Most of the time after dinner when he wasn't doing homework or working on his basketball journal, he either wanted to watch a game, or read a book.

"I can't believe you read when you don't have to," Ryan had said to him one time.

"It's fun," Lucas said.

"Dude," Ryan said, "you have some weird ideas about having fun."

Tonight, though, he was online, trying to get into what his mom called the way-back machine, and see if he could get any information about Sam Winston's basketball career. He didn't think of it as going behind Gramps's back. But his mom was right. He *was* curious.

So he typed in "Sam Winston" and "basketball."

There had been plenty of basketball players with the name "Winston," first or last, but no player with that full name. There were a couple baseball players, and a football player.

Nothing for a basketball player with Gramps's name.

So Lucas took a deeper dive. He typed in the name and typed in "basketball" and then "California" and "1960s," which is when Gramps would have played college ball.

Still nothing.

It occurred to him that Gramps had played so little, wherever he had played, that there wasn't a record of him having played at all in the way-back machine, especially at a school he said had gone out of business. Lucas was starting to think that maybe he wasn't working on a biography at all, but a mystery.

But Lucas wasn't giving up, not yet. He pictured himself in the gym or at Westley Park, and all the hours he'd spent putting in extra hours on his shot.

For now, he took one last try.

He typed in "California colleges that closed."

Except that just made him even more confused, because of the long list that came up, not just including colleges that had closed in the past, but some that had merged with other colleges over time, becoming brand-new schools with new names.

He sighed and closed his laptop. His mom happened to be walking past his doorway when he did. Lucas heard her laugh.

"I thought a gust of wind must have just blown into your room," she said. "But then I realized that sound had come out of my son."

He told her what he'd been doing.

"Slow going?" she said.

"The slowest," he said. "I can't find anything that tells me that Gramps ever even *played* college ball."

"I know this is going to shock you," she said, "but Google doesn't know everything about everybody."

"You probably found that on Google," Lucas said, grinning at her.

"In the world of new information," she said, "a lot of stuff can still slip through the cracks."

"I don't want new information," he said. "Just looking for old news here."

She came in and rested a hand on his shoulder and squeezed.

"Eventually you might have to do it the old-fashioned way," she said.

"What's that?"

"Go to the source."

"Gramps," he said.

"Yes, sir."

"But what if he hasn't changed his mind?" Lucas said.

"Then," his mom said, "as important as doing this paper on him is to you, what he wants will be more important."

TEN

They lucked into some free gym time after school the next afternoon, so Lucas and some of the other guys from the Wolves got to play some three-on-three. Even when the game ended, Lucas stayed on and worked on his game alone, because there was still forty-five minutes before his mom was going to pick him up. Mr. Collins had supervised the three-on-three game, sitting in the bleachers as he graded papers. Before he went back to his classroom, he gave Lucas the key to the equipment closet, telling him to put the ball back when he was through, lock the closet, and drop off the key with him.

"I promised your mother I wouldn't let you just wander around the school by yourself," Mr. Collins said.

"When I've got the gym all to myself?" Lucas said. "Yeah, like *that's* going to happen."

Today Lucas went to all the spots on the court where Gramps's offense was likely to take him, and shot the ball from there. He worked on his left-handed dribble, going end to end using his left hand exclusively, finishing each trip up the court with a left-handed drive to the basket. He shot free throws until he could make ten in a row. If he missed, even on the last one, he'd start all over again. Even after having played a hard three-on-three game, he didn't feel tired. He was exactly where he wanted to be.

When he finished, he still had a few minutes before his mom was scheduled to arrive. Lucas put his ball back in the equipment closet, locked it behind him as he'd told Mr. Collins he would, and headed down the hall for Mr. C.'s classroom.

Before he got there, he heard the piano music, and knew it had to be Maria in the music room.

He had no idea what song she was playing. It sounded like something serious. But it was good. Really good.

Sometimes when Lucas's mom would watch basketball with him, she would freely admit that she didn't appreciate the subtle aspects of the game the way Lucas and Gramps did. But she always knew which players were doing things that the other players weren't.

It was that way for Lucas when Maria was playing the piano. Maybe someday he'd appreciate the music she could play. He'd heard other classmates in the music room. What Maria was doing was different. Better.

He quietly pushed the door open, so as not to disturb her. He had a perfect view of her face, and could see that as serious as the music was, she was smiling.

This, he thought, *is her court.*

This was Maria alone with her music the way Lucas had just been alone with basketball.

When she finished, he couldn't help himself. He started to applaud. The sound didn't startle her. It just made her smile get bigger as she turned on the bench to face him.

"Sneak," she said.

"Am not," he said.

"You snuck up on me, one hundred percent," she said.

"You're not supposed to make noise when you're in the audi-ence," Lucas said.

"Well," she said, "clearly you snuck in without a ticket."

"It's not free?" he said.

"Just for today," she said. "Next time I'm charging you."

"I know I've told you this before," he said. "But you're really good."

"I can do better," she said.

"It sounded perfect to me," Lucas said.

"I could explain why it wasn't and the places where I messed up," she said. "But it would be like you trying to explain all the things that happened in your game the other day."

Maria said her mom was on her way to school to pick her up. They agreed to wait together out front.

"How's your paper coming?" she said as they walked toward Mr. Collins's classroom.

"I was afraid you were going to ask me that."

"Why?"

"Because it's not coming."

She waited while he knocked on Mr. Collins's door. Mr. C. was working with Cissy Sullivan, another seventh grader. Lucas just showed him he was leaving the equipment key on a back desk, and said he'd see him tomorrow, and left.

"What do you mean the paper isn't going anywhere?" Maria said.

"My grandfather doesn't want me to make it about him," Lucas said.

"Why not?"

"He hasn't really made that clear," Lucas said. "What he *has* made pretty clear is that he wants me to find another subject."

"*Are* you going to find another subject?"

"Not yet," he said. "If I have to, I might ask Mr. Collins if I could do it about him. But I'm not ready to give up on Gramps. I still think it's a cool idea. It's my way of putting down the feelings I have for him in my heart down on paper."

"He's such a cool guy," Maria said. "I was watching him watch you during the game on Saturday. He looked like the happiest person in the world."

"I want this paper to make him happy," Lucas said.

"You'll figure it out."

"How do you figure?" Lucas said.

Maria smiled again. Lucas would never admit this to Ryan, or even his mom. But he thought she had an amazing smile.

"Hey," she said. "You're the writer."

ELEVEN

The Sheridan Sonics hadn't been one of the better sixth-grade teams last year, but had certainly been the biggest.

Their center, Robbie Marino, had been the tallest player in the Twin Lakes League, by a lot. And when they showed up at the gym at the Sheridan YMCA, they saw that Robbie had just continued to grow.

"I was hoping that he'd gotten shorter somehow," Ryan said to Lucas.

"Don't worry, you showed last season you can guard that guy," Lucas said. "And I know you can do it again." He paused. "If the refs allow you to stand on a chair."

"Is that your idea of a pep talk?" Ryan said. "Seriously?"

"No," Lucas said. "That was just me trying to lighten your mood. Or your load."

"That guy *is* a load," Ryan said.

"I'll try to do better," Lucas said. He grinned. "But that sounds like a pretty tall order."

"You're not funny," Ryan said.

"You *know* I'm funny," Lucas said. "It's just that right now you don't *think* I'm funny."

Ryan was still staring at Robbie, shaking his head slowly and sadly.

"Don't worry," Lucas said. "You just stay between him and the basket as much as you can. And I'll drop off and help out whenever I can, same as we did last year when we shut them down."

"I don't know why I even have to guard him," Ryan said. "He's their center and Billy's ours."

"Gramps told me he likes your quickness staying in front of him," Lucas said. "And how long you are."

"You know what's really going to be long?" Ryan said. "This day."

"You want my real pep talk?" Lucas said. "He's bigger. You're better. End of speech."

MIKE LUPICA

He thought that Gramps had been quieter than usual on the twenty-minute ride from Claremont to Sheridan. But Lucas had to remind himself that Gramps did tire sometimes, that he did act his age, especially if the pain in his knees had prevented him from getting a good night's sleep.

He just hoped that the closer they got to the game, the more Gramps's disposition would improve. And that's exactly what had happened by the time he gathered the Wolves around him in front of their bench, a few minutes before the ref would hand Lucas the ball.

"Just gonna give you boys one thought before we start today," Gramps said, smiling his Santa Claus smile. "You all can handle one thought, right?"

"Unless we count that question as a second thought," Ryan said.

Gramps raised an eyebrow and looked at Lucas.

"The truly amazing thing," he said to Gramps, "is that he actually thinks he's funnier than me."

"I'm just trying to keep my mind off guarding a guy who looks as big as Zion Williamson," Ryan said.

"Anyway," Gramps said, "here's the thought: Let's not wait until the second quarter to start playing our best ball this Saturday the way we did last Saturday."

The Wolves didn't.

This Saturday they came out hot. Smoking hot. And it all started with their defense. Ryan made it his mission not just to stay in front of Robbie, but to bother him in every way he could, whether he had the ball in his hands or not. Every chance he got, he forced Robbie into one of Lucas's double teams. He boxed him out on missed shots at both ends of the court, beating Robbie to his spot time after time as a way of beating him to the ball.

Every once in a while Robbie would reach over him and come out with the ball.

Not very often.

Ryan had told Lucas that he didn't care if he scored a single point today. He wasn't going to let the big guy beat them. But Ryan did get his points, mostly because of the outlet passes he was making, and the way he kept busting it to fill lanes on the fast break.

The Wolves were ahead by ten points at the end of the first quarter. They were ahead by fifteen at halftime. Up and down their lineup, no matter which five was on the court at a particular time, they looked exactly like the team Lucas had imagined they would be coming into the season. It wasn't just Ryan on defense; they were all D-ing up, all over the court. They were sharing the ball on offense, and making their share of shots from the outside, starting with Lucas, who'd even made one over Robbie when Robbie had his arms in the air and looked as tall as a Christmas tree.

Lucas had a pretty good idea about how many assists he had by halftime. But in the end, he never cared about his own stats. Gramps had always drummed into his head that the only stat that mattered for a point guard wasn't a number. It was a letter:

W.

For wins.

He still knew he had a boatload of assists today. And also knew that at the half, everybody who'd been in the game for the Wolves had at least one basket.

All Gramps said to them at halftime was this:

"Keep doing what you're doing. You're making me look like a genius."

The Wolves slowed things down in the second half once it became clear that the Sonics were never going to cut into their lead. They stopped fast-breaking. They ran more set plays on offense, and worked more clock. Nobody wanted to embarrass the Sonics. Gramps always told them to imagine what it would feel like to be on the other side of a beatdown like this. By the start of the fourth quarter they had proved, in just about every way, that they were the better team today. There was no need to rub it in.

Gramps always talked about playing the game right. This

was what that felt like. He always said if you did enough things right, the results would take care of themselves. And so they had against the Sonics.

The best result? They walked off the court 2–0.

If last Saturday had been a great day because of the way they had come back, this one felt ever sweeter. They hadn't just shown the Sonics the kind of basketball of which they were capable.

They'd shown themselves.

You couldn't ask for more than that, especially this early in the season. Couldn't ask for a better day.

Until dinner that night.

TWELVE

Lucas couldn't have drawn things up better if he were drawing up a perfect play: win over Sheridan, mom's meatloaf for dinner with banana splits all around for dessert, then the Warriors vs. the Thunder on television, which meant Steph Curry against Chris Paul at point guard. Gramps said it would be like taking a master class in playing the position, at least when James Harden wasn't dribbling the darn ball.

At dinner they went over all the highlights of the Wolves and Sonics game. The conversation nearly taking them all the way to banana splits because there had *been* so many highlights.

Gramps said the thing he'd liked the best was how disciplined Lucas and his teammates had stayed even after the game became a blowout, none of them slacking off, all of them still looking to make the extra pass, and sometimes one more pass after that.

"When it's like that," Gramps says, "teamwork never *feels* like work."

"Maybe it's because of all the work we put in at practice," Lucas said.

"It's got a chance to be a special group," Lucas's grandfather said.

Julia Winston smiled. "I hear that it might have a little something to do with a pretty special coach."

"Wouldn't matter who the coach was if they didn't want to listen, and these boys listen," he said. "Not a chowderhead in the bunch. Certainly not the kind of chowderhead I was when I was young."

"Not possible," Lucas said.

Gramps was quiet for a moment, with a faraway look that he would get sometimes, like a cloud passing across his face.

"Least I learned from my mistakes," he said. "When the boy finally did become a man."

"Or when a girl becomes a woman," Lucas's mom said, smiling again. "Glad I learned from all the mistakes *I* made when I was young."

After dessert, and after they'd all cleaned up the kitchen, the three of them went into the living room to watch the game. Lucas's mom said that even she was excited to see Steph Curry and Chris Paul get after each other.

"Though," she said to Gramps, "after watching our boy this morning, I bet those guys could pick up a few pointers from him."

"Now you're talking crazy talk," Lucas said.

"Someday," she said to him, "people will be watching you on TV on a Saturday night."

"In your dreams," Lucas said to her. "Or maybe mine."

"I'm good either way," she said.

The Warriors and Thunder were tied at the half. Lucas's mom said she was going into the kitchen to make popcorn. When she'd left the room Lucas said to his grandfather, "Ask you something?"

"Ask me anything except to explain how the Thunder could possibly have left the best shooter in the game wide-open for that three right before the buzzer," he said.

Lucas took a deep breath, let it out. Slowly.

"I want to ask you again to help me out with the paper about you I want to do for school," he said.

"Back to that, are we?" Gramps said.

He grinned.

"Yeah," Lucas said. "We are."

"I'd still rather you wouldn't," Gramps said.

"I don't understand," Lucas said.

"And for a good coach," Gramps said, "I'm not doing much of a job at making you understand."

"I want to know what kind of player you were," Lucas said.

"Just one who didn't get the most out of his potential, the way you do," Gramps said.

"Well, that's pretty hard for me to believe," Lucas said.

"Believe it," Gramps said. "And thinking about it makes me sad, even though I don't think about it very much."

"I'd never want to make you sad," Lucas said.

Gramps had his back to the kitchen. Lucas saw his mom quietly come into the room with a big bowl of popcorn, then just as quietly turn and go back into the kitchen. Even though she'd offered to help, it was as if she understood that this was something between Lucas and his grandfather, at least for now.

"I don't even know where you went to college," Lucas said. "I don't even know for sure whether you played point guard or not."

"I was a guard," Gramps said in a soft voice. "In those days, you weren't a point guard or a shooting guard. You were just a guard."

"See!" Lucas said, excited all of a sudden. "See right there!

That would be a great point for me to make in the paper."

"I never say no to you, son," Gramps said. "Just let me do it this one time, and we can just devote ourselves to the season you're playing, and not ones I played a million years ago."

"Maybe you need to respect your grandfather's wishes on this," she said, "as much as they might disappoint you."

Lucas understood what his mom was saying. He understood that she was right. He knew he was being more stubborn than ever. And he didn't want Gramps to think they were having an argument about this. They'd never argued about anything.

"I just wanted to know more about you, Gramps," Lucas said.

"But that's the thing," Gramps said. "You *do* know me."

"Didn't my dad want to know more about what you were like when you were younger?" Lucas said.

A sad look came across Gramps's face, but then it disappeared as quickly as it had come.

"I just used to tell him what I'm going to tell you now," he said. "That he was seeing my best self, and that's all that should matter to him."

Gramps stood up. It only took him one try this time to get off the couch. He came over and patted the top of Lucas's head and said, "Time for me to go. If the weather's warm enough tomorrow, maybe the two of us can go to the park."

"Okay," Lucas said.

In that moment there was nothing else for him *to* say. The park was a way for his grandfather to change the subject. Lucas's mom told Gramps to drive carefully. He thanked her again for dinner. A couple minutes later they heard his car pull out of the driveway.

"I know that didn't end the way you wanted it to," Lucas's mom said. "But he's still the best man we know. And you *do* see the best in him."

Then Lucas told his mom what he'd been thinking the last couple days, that he couldn't help thinking this had somehow turned into a mystery.

"Maybe to you," she said. "Just not to your grandfather."

THIRTEEN

After changing his mind a few times, Ryan at least came up with his subject for the paper:

His tennis coach, Mr. Nichols.

There was no tennis team at Claremont Middle School. But there was a summer team at Claremont Country Club, where his family had a membership. And from the time Ryan had joined, he really had been better at tennis than basketball. He was a great natural athlete and, because he was so long, had a powerful serve that seemed to explode down out of the sky at his opponents.

He'd never loved baseball, or lacrosse, the sport Lucas played in the spring and then into the summer with his travel team. But he needed a sport to keep him occupied in the summer. What he did love to do was compete.

The problem was, when he'd started playing matches, he competed way *too* hard. As intense as he was when he was playing on a team, it was worse when he was alone on a tennis court, when it was just him and his opponent. He'd even broken a racket one time, and gotten defaulted out of the semifinals of a tournament it looked like he was about to win.

Mr. Nichols taught Ryan to channel his emotions in a positive way. He got him playing tennis all year round, and to appreciate what it was like in sports when the only teammate on whom you could rely was yourself. So Ryan would play tournaments in the area in the fall, and then in the spring, and all the way into the summer. He also came to love working with Mr. Nichols, the way Lucas loved working with Gramps.

Ryan was in Lucas's room on Sunday afternoon when he told him he'd decided on Mr. Nichols as a subject. He asked how it was going with Lucas and Gramps, and Lucas told him he'd decided to move on to a new subject himself, and would probably end up writing about Mr. Collins.

"I'd still rather do one on Gramps," Lucas said, "but not if he doesn't want me to. And he *really* doesn't want me to."

"I know Mr. Collins isn't as important in your life as your Gramps is," Ryan said. "But I'm sure you'll write a great paper." He grinned. "But before you do that, you have to help me at least write a good one, because I feel like it's match point against me if I don't."

Ryan suddenly grabbed his head with his hands. "I just can't get a C!" he said. "That's the deal. I keep thinking I could get my mom to slide a little bit on this, because she was a player once. But my dad isn't budging."

Ryan's dad was the principal at Claremont High School. He was a really good guy, and Lucas knew he was a good dad. But he was as serious about education as Ryan's mom had been about basketball when she was a star for the UConn women's team.

"You know how we call Claremont Country Club 'The Triple C'?" Ryan said. "Well, that's all the Cs I'm allowed."

"You're not a C student," Lucas said, "even in English. C'mon, dude. You got this. *We* got this."

"Writing comes easy to you," Ryan said.

"Nope," Lucas said. "I have to work at it like everybody else. You just have to stop telling yourself you can't."

"But that's the thing," Ryan said. "I really can't!"

"Yeah, dude, you can," Lucas said. He grinned again. "When you're serving in tennis, what's the best way to win a big point?"

"Ace," Ryan said.

"So stop talking about Cs," Lucas said. "And let's ace English."

It took a while for Ryan to get going. As much as he liked to talk, and he *really* liked to talk, he often had trouble organizing his thoughts. So Lucas asked him to just go back to the beginning of his relationship with Mr. Nichols. As Ryan talked, Lucas sat at his laptop and wrote down what he was saying.

"I'm not going to write your paper for you," Lucas said. "But if you can just see how some of it looks on the page, I think it might help you."

"Then I can put it into my words," Ryan said.

Lucas shook his head.

"No," Lucas said. "These are already your words. When I'm done, and you look at this first draft, it will be your job to put them into complete sentences. And *really* make it sound like you."

"You're the one who should be an English teacher," Ryan said.

"Nah," Lucas said. "Not even close. That's Mr. C.'s job. I'm just trying to give you a different kind of assist here."

"But what if I hoist up an airball?" Ryan said.

"Dude," Lucas said. "You gotta lose this attitude. If Gramps heard you talking like that, you'd never get off the bench."

They went back to work. Ryan kept talking about why he

loved tennis and how Mr. Nichols had made him love it even more. As he talked, Lucas tried to keep up with his typing, not worrying about making mistakes, just wanting to get down the important parts of what Ryan was saying. When Ryan finished talking, Lucas went back over what he'd written, cleaned it up, made it into three paragraphs, and printed it out for him.

"Can I tell you one more thing?" Lucas said.

"How to get the grade I need?" Ryan said. "That would work."

"No," Lucas said. "Don't put off writing this thing until the last minute. Write a little bit every day. That will take the pressure off."

"Nothing is going to take the pressure off!"

Lucas grinned.

"Weren't we just talking about an attitude adjustment?" he said.

"Can't I just borrow yours?" Ryan said.

"Don't think it works that way," Lucas said.

He asked if Ryan wanted to stay for dinner, saying he'd already cleared it with his mom. Ryan said he couldn't, his grandparents were coming over to his house for dinner. Lucas walked downstairs to the front door. Before Ryan left, they pounded fists.

"You're the dude," Ryan said.

"You'd do the same for me," Lucas said.

"You don't quit," Ryan said.

"Never," Lucas said.

It's why the next day he planned to go through the boxes in the attic.

FOURTEEN

When Lucas's mom hadn't finished her classes by the time Claremont Middle dismissed its students—something that usually only happened two days a week—one of his mom's students would stay at the house until Lucas's mom did come home.

Lucas's favorite babysitter, even though he refused to ever call her that, was Lucy McQuade. She was more like an older sister. She was a sophomore at St. Luke's College, and wanted to be a writer. When Lucy was in the house, she'd usually sit at the kitchen table doing her schoolwork and Lucas would go upstairs and do his, especially if he had basketball practice later.

But he didn't do homework the next afternoon after school. He told Lucy that he was going upstairs to poke around in his dad's old stuff up there.

"Is it okay with your mom?" Lucy said.

"Yeah," Lucas said. "My mom hardly ever goes up there anymore, because I think it just makes her sad, even though she says she's never going to get rid of those boxes. But sometimes when I'm up there, I just feel as if I'm hanging with him for a few minutes."

Lucy looked at Lucas over the screen of her laptop.

"I'm sure those boxes are full of some very nice memories," she said.

"Sometimes even the nice ones make me sad," Lucas said.

Even though they called it an attic, it wasn't spooky or full of cobwebs. There was a small window that faced the backyard and let a fair amount of sun in. And Lucas's mom, being his mom, had kept everything neat and organized. There was even a desk had belonged to his dad.

Sometimes Lucas would bring his laptop up and sit at the desk and write, and imagine his dad, the one he only knew through everybody else's memories, looking over his shoulder.

Boxes lined the walls. A few of them had clothes in them, old basketball jerseys, even his dad's varsity letter jacket from when he'd played for Claremont High. The box with the letter jacket in it had a picture of his dad wearing it, with his arm around Lucas's mom. They looked happy in that picture.

They had started dating in high school, and his mom had always said, "We never really stopped."

There were a lot of boxes filled with textbooks from med school. Lucas wasn't sure why his mom kept them. But she did, along with some old black-and-white composition books filled with his dad's handwriting, most of which Lucas could barely read. He wasn't one to talk, of course. His handwriting wasn't much to look at either.

There were a couple boxes with his dad's trophies, going all the way back to when he played seventh-trade travel basketball, all bubble-wrapped for safekeeping. There were some cool photographs of Michael Winston at that age, looking a lot like Lucas.

Lucas picked up one now, and felt himself starting to tear up, the way he did sometimes when he was up here alone with the pictures and trophies and memories.

It wasn't just the pictures of Lucas's dad and his mom when they were younger. He always looked happy in the pictures, no matter what age he was. If it was a team picture, Michael Winston's smile was always the biggest one.

The tears went away. His dad looked too happy. Lucas smiled.

He knew from Gramps, and from his mom, that his dad had been some player before he tore up his knee. His mom had put together a scrapbook with old clippings from the Claremont paper about his dad's career. Lucas had read the story about the night his dad had gotten injured, making a steal at the end of a game against Sheridan that saved that game for Claremont. There was a picture with the story showing two of his dad's teammates helping him off the court.

Gramps was right behind them.

It brought Lucas back to why he'd come up here today. He just wanted to see if there was anything about Gramps he'd missed when he'd been alone up here with these boxes. He wanted to see if there was something, or anything, that would provide even a little information about him. All the other times Lucas had been in the attic, it was almost as if he were visiting his dad's childhood. He'd never been up here trying to learn about Gramps. Now he wished there was a box with Gramps's stuff in it. Only there wasn't. There was nothing up here to tell Lucas about what Gramps's life had been like when he was a boy growing up in California.

Maybe Lucas should have started asking him questions about that long before this. Or maybe if he had, the answers would have been the same as they were now, which meant no answers at all. All Lucas knew for sure was that by the time his dad had been born, his grandfather and grandmother were living in Claremont.

"C'mon, Gramps," Lucas said out loud. "Help a guy out here."

He decided to open up one more box. It was the one with his dad's Chip Hilton books in it. These were the books that had been Michael Winston's favorites when he was Lucas's age, and loved to read as much as Lucas did now. Lucas knew this because his mom had told him, telling him all the time about how these books in particular were most meaningful to him. By now, Lucas had read most of them too. They were about a star athlete named Chip Hilton, who'd grown up in a town called Valley Falls before he and his buddies went off to college. He played football and basketball and baseball, and the books would go from sport to sport and season to season. When Lucas was little, his mom would read Chip Hilton books called *Championship Ball* and *Hardcourt Upset* and *A Pass and a Prayer* as his bedtime stories. Lucas loved them all.

"These are the books that made you love to read before you could read," his mom told him one time.

He was holding *Hardcourt Upset* in his hands when a picture fell out of it.

There were two basketball players in it.

It was obviously an old picture, Lucas could tell that just by looking at the uniforms. He couldn't believe how small and tight the shorts looked. One player wore number 14. One wore number 24. There were holding the same basketball between them. Both the players had their hair buzzed really, really short.

Bisons was written across the front of their jerseys.

Lucas turned over the photograph. On the back was written a date: 10/15/61. Underneath the date were two names: Joe and Tommy.

They were standing underneath a basket, but there was nothing around them that identified the gym. It could have been any gym anywhere. Lucas couldn't even tell for sure whether they were high school players or college players.

Both of them were smiling.

But who were they?

Why had his dad kept this picture?

Joe who? Lucas thought.

Tommy who?

He'd come up here looking for answers, and now just had more questions.

FIFTEEN

He took the picture with him down to his room. While Lucas waited for his mom to get home he opened his laptop, went to Google, and typed in, "Colleges with nickname or mascot Bisons."

A bunch of them came up.

There was Bethany College in West Virginia. Bucknell in Pennsylvania. A university called Harding. Howard. North Dakota State. Oklahoma Baptist. Lucas didn't know if they all had basketball teams, but assumed they did, because just about all colleges did.

Did one of them, the guy on the left, look a little like his dad?

Lucas couldn't ever remember seeing a picture of Gramps at that age. But because of the date on the back of the picture, if the guy on the left did look like Michael Winston, it could have been Sam Winston in 1961.

But it didn't mean that it was. Lucas's mom would show him pictures of her from college, when she had a *lot* more hair than she did now, and even though he knew it was her, he wasn't sure if he would have been able to pick her out of a class picture.

10/15/61.

Joe and Tommy.

Number 14 and number 24.

If they were college players, that meant the season was about to start in October, if the calendar for college hoops was the same then as it was now. Gramps would have played his college ball about that time.

But these guys were named Joe and Tommy.

If one of them *wasn't* Gramps, why in the world had his dad held on to a picture of them? Maybe Gramps had stuck the picture in there a long time ago, even though Lucas couldn't imagine why. Maybe these guys had been teammates of his, on a team called the Bisons.

Maybe, Lucas thought, he should just take the picture back

up to the attic and put it back in the book and do exactly what his mom had suggested he do. Just move on. Leave this alone. Leave Gramps with his own memories, both good and bad. Maybe he should focus his energy on basketball and his journal and his paper on Mr. Collins, and do something else his mom had suggested he do and respect his grandfather's wishes.

As confusing as everything had become, he didn't want one school paper to come between him and Gramps. What was the point of that? He knew how special their relationship had always been. He knew how important that relationship was to him, and to Gramps, too. He didn't know if Gramps would even want to keep coaching after this season. Lucas could see him slowing down, as enthusiastic as he still was about teaching. So if this was going to be their last season together, Lucas knew that his real energy—and his positive energy—ought to go into making it as special as possible.

Gramps talked constantly about playing the right way. Maybe moving on, and respecting his wishes—maybe leaving the past in the past—was a way for Lucas to do the right thing. Or maybe, just maybe, this was a picture Gramps had lost a long time ago, or one more thing he'd forgotten, and Lucas would be doing him a favor by showing it to him.

He'd have to think about that. In this case, he wasn't sure what the right play was.

First he went downstairs and started to prepare their dinner salad, something he'd promised her he would do before they both left for school in the morning. He cleaned the lettuce, cut up some radishes and carrots and cucumbers. His mom liked to joke that he was on his way to one of those chef shows on television.

When she got home, he went upstairs, got the picture of Joe and Tommy off his desk, and brought it down for her to look at.

Her first reaction was to giggle, before looking at it closely.

"How did players manage to even run up and down the court in shorts that tight?" she said. "They looked like the basketball version of tighty whities."

"I kind of thought the same thing," he said. "But that's kind of not why I'm showing you the picture."

"Figured," she said.

"Why would Dad stick an old picture of two guys named Joe and Tommy in one of his old Chip Hilton books?"

"No idea."

"Is Gramps coming over for dinner tonight?" Lucas said.

"Probably not," she said. "He always calls first and he hasn't called today. You know him. Polite to a fault."

They were seated at the table. She was waiting for water to boil so she could start cooking the pasta she was going to serve with chicken and broccoli. She picked up the photograph, really studying it now, frowning. Then she got up from the table suddenly and said she'd be right back.

When she came back, she was holding a picture of a young guy who looked like the Bisons' player on the left. He had longer hair, slicked back, looking black in the black-and-white picture. But he resembled the player on the left.

A lot.

She placed that picture next to Lucas's on the table.

"Did you find that one in the attic, too?" Lucas said.

"No," she said. "It was in my room. In a little box of old pictures I keep in my closet that I haven't looked at in a long time."

"You know one of those guys?" Lucas said.

"I do," Julia said. "The one on the left."

"Who is he?"

"Gramps," she said.

SIXTEEN

Okay," Lucas said to his mom. "This makes *no* sense."

"I can't say for sure that it's your grandfather," she said. "But except for the hair, they could be twins."

"I never saw that picture before," Lucas said.

"I didn't even remember I had it," Julia said. "Pretty sure it's the only one I've got of your grandfather as a young man. The ones with him and your dad, he's a lot older, obviously."

"Could Gramps have had a brother named Joe or Tommy?" Lucas said.

"Your dad didn't have any uncles or aunts," Lucas's mom

said. "And at our wedding, the only family on your dad's side was Gramps and your grandmom."

Lucas reached down and moved the pictures around, just to be doing something with his hands.

"Where is Gramps from in California?" Lucas said.

"The few times I ever talked about this with your dad," she said, "he just said that his dad had been a foster child, and moved around a lot when he was a boy. I think he mentioned Bakersfield. Maybe Fresno. One time in particular I asked your dad, 'Aren't you curious about what your dad's life was like growing up?' And he kind of shrugged and said that Gramps didn't like talking about it. He just assumed it hadn't been a particularly happy childhood, that going from one family to another had been like having no real family at all."

"And you never asked Gramps yourself?"

"You know him," she said. "He talks about what he wants to talk about. Like he's calling the plays even when you're having a conversation with him."

Lucas said, "Maybe I don't know him nearly as well as I thought I did."

The Wolves' next practice was the following night, the first of two practices before they'd play the Grisham Mavs the Saturday after next. Lucas had been excited from the time he'd seen the schedule and realized this would be their third game. He was going to get the chance to go up against Jake Farr, who'd been one of the best point guards in their league last year. Jake was the Twin Lakes League version of Steph Curry, because of the way Jake could handle the ball and make shots from just about everywhere. He'd been a little taller than Lucas when they were sixth-graders, just as fast, left-handed. A total star. Lucas couldn't wait.

Tonight they worked a lot on their transition defense. If the Mavs hadn't changed their style, they liked to run as much as the Wolves did. So Gramps had a chance tonight to talk about one of his favorite subjects: turning good defense into offense.

"No matter how fast they come at you," he said, "you can always slow those boys down with good D. You make them miss. You make them rush. You take the ball away. And then it's *you* coming at *them* fast. Like you're trying to give those poor boys a case of whiplash."

Being even more aggressive on defense than the other guys were on offense was another big thing with Gramps.

"I don't want you to be afraid to take chances, or make mistakes," he said. "Everybody makes mistakes in this world, and not just in basketball. The best you can do is keep taking chances, and hope not to make the same mistake twice. The great Red Auerbach used to tell his shooters, 'If you miss a few, keep shooting.'"

At the end of practice they scrimmaged less than usual. Lucas had no problem with that, either. This was the best way for them to get their minds right for the Grisham Mavs. It was another example of what a good coach Gramps was, Lucas thought. *He could get a bunch of twelve-year olds this fired up about defense.*

Lucas's mom had asked Gramps to drive him home when they were finished. Before they headed for the parking lot, Lucas helped Gramps collect the basketballs and the pinnies they'd used for the scrimmage.

The other players were gone by then. It was just the two of them in the gym. It had been an early practice. It was just a few minutes past seven.

"You coming for dinner?" Lucas said to his grandfather. "Mom's making turkey burgers."

"I do love those turkey burgers your mom makes," Gramps said.

"So you're in?"

"Already told that to the best cook in Claremont."

He smiled. Lucas smiled back at him.

"Ask you something?" Lucas said.

"In my life," Gramps said, "I don't think I've ever met a boy as full of questions as my grandson."

"How else am I gonna learn?" Lucas said. "That's what my coach is always telling me, anyway."

Lucas's backpack was on the floor near the bleachers where he'd dropped it before practice. He went over and unzipped a side pouch and took out the picture of Joe and Tommy and brought it with him to where Gramps was standing at mid court, car keys already in his hand.

"I want to show you something I found in one of Dad's old Chip Hilton books," Lucas said.

He handed his grandfather the picture.

Gramps took it. Lucas could see the slight tremor in his hands, but there was nothing unusual about that. Gramps just called it one more old-man thing he had to deal with. Lucas would notice it sometimes when he was lifting a drinking glass, or holding a piece of paper up to show Lucas a new play.

He studied the picture before handing it back to Lucas.

"What did you want to ask me?" he said.

"I wanted to ask you if that's you in the picture," Lucas said. "Mom thinks it might be."

"Tell me again how you found it," Gramps said.

"I wasn't looking for it, I promise," Lucas said. "It just fell out of a book in the attic."

"What were you doing up there?" Gramps said.

"You know I go up there sometimes," Lucas said. "I like going through Dad's stuff."

Suddenly he felt as if he were back playing defense, and wasn't sure why. Or what to say.

"You *are* stubborn," Gramps said.

"Mom says I get it from you."

"Probably so."

"So is that you?" Lucas said.

"More like who I used to be," Gramps said.

"Joe or Tommy?" Lucas said.

Gramps took a deep breath, let it out.

"They called me Joe back in the day," he said.

Then he said, "Time to take you home."

Without another word he turned and led Lucas out of the gym and to the place in the front parking lot where his car was. They both got in. Gramps drove them home.

Lucas was afraid to say anything himself until they were in his driveway. It was as if Gramps's silence had formed this force field around him. But when the car stopped Lucas said, "Are you still going to have dinner?"

"I'm awful tired all of a sudden," he said. "Think I might turn in early tonight. Please make my apologies to your mom."

Lucas got out of the car, but didn't close the door.

"Are you okay, Gramps?" he asked.

"Sure," he said. "Just tired, like I said. Some days I feel all my years more than others."

Because the door was open, the interior lights in the car were on, so Lucas could see clearly the look on his grandfather's face. For a second, Lucas thought Gramps was the one who might start to cry.

In a soft voice Lucas said, "Why'd they call you Joe?"

He wasn't sure his grandfather had heard him correctly, because he didn't answer the question.

"He's just a boy who got left behind a long time ago," he said. He took another deep breath and let it out slowly. Then asked Lucas to please close the door.

"Good night, son," Gramps said.

He drove away. Lucas stood there in the driveway and watched him go, wondering in that moment why "good night" had sounded so much like "good-bye."

SEVENTEEN

Lucas's mom tried to call Gramps when Lucas told her what had happened at the gym. Gramps didn't answer his phone. That wasn't unusual. Gramps had finally given in and purchased a cell phone, but he preferred talking on the landline at his apartment.

She was sent to voice mail on his cell. She got the answering machine at his apartment.

"He really didn't talk all the way home?" Lucas's mom said.

Lucas shook his head.

"He said they called him Joe?"

"Yes."

"But didn't explain why?"

"No."

They were in his mom's room. She was up there reading when Gramps dropped off Lucas. Now he was sitting on the end of his mom's bed. He still had the picture of Joe and Tommy in his hand.

"Gramps was Joe," he said. "Now he's Sam." He groaned. "I really do wish I'd never started asking questions in the first place."

"Now the genie is out of the bottle," she said. "And I'm not exactly sure how we get it back inside."

"If I had dropped this when Gramps asked me to," Lucas said, "none of this would have happened."

"Sometimes not giving up has consequences," his mom said.

"I know," Lucas said. It came out of him like a groan. "I feel like going to my room and doing a deep dive under the covers and just wait for this to be over."

She patted the space next to her on the bed. Lucas went and sat there. She put her arm around him. "It doesn't seem like it right now," she said. "But this will all work itself out."

"I feel like I'm about to mess up our whole season," he said.

"You know that's not going to happen," she said. "Basketball is too important to both of you. Let's just give him some room to breathe. When's your next practice?"

"Thursday," he said. "And you wait and see. I won't see Gramps until then. I'll bet you anything he doesn't come to dinner tomorrow night, either."

"You give yourself some room to breathe, too," she said. "Go watch a game. Read a book. Do some writing. Let's see what happens at practice. Maybe I'll go with you if you're worried about things being too awkward. We'll *all* get through this together."

Gramps wasn't at practice Thursday night. Mrs. Moretti, who'd been away doing some alumni work for the UConn women's basketball program, told Lucas and his teammates that Gramps had called her that afternoon and asked if she'd mind taking over for him.

Ryan poked Lucas and whispered, "Did you know this was going to happen?"

"Nope." Lucas turned to Ryan's mom and said, "Did Gramps say anything about not feeling well? He never misses a practice."

"He didn't," Jen Moretti said. "Just said he had some personal business to take care of."

"Did he say what kind?" Lucas said.

"I actually thought you might know," she said, grinning, "since neither one of you seems to make a move without the other one knowing."

"No idea," Lucas said. "He didn't mention anything to my mom or to me."

Gramps hadn't said *anything* to either one of them, because he hadn't returned any calls since Tuesday night.

When Mrs. Moretti dropped him off after practice, Lucas told his mom about Gramps not being at practice.

She immediately pulled her phone out of the back pocket of her jeans and tried to call Gramps again.

"Voice mail."

Then she hit a few more keys on her phone and shook her head and said, "Answering machine."

"We should drive over there and make sure he's okay," Lucas said.

Julia motioned for Lucas to pump the brakes.

"He was fine when he called Jen," she said. "Maybe he just wants some of that space we talked about. And let's be honest, if he wanted to talk to us right now he'd be talking to us, because there's nothing stopping him."

"Except being stubborn," Lucas said, then added, "Stubborn as me."

"We don't know the whole story," she said.

"And don't know if Dad knew."

"Your dad and I never kept many secrets from each other," she said. "So if he was keeping one about Gramps, he must have had his reasons."

"You think Gramps *will* ever tell us the whole story?" Lucas said.

"I know you don't want to hear this," she said. "But he might not."

"And you know what?" Lucas said. "I'd be okay with that, no lie."

"All you did was ask a question," his mom said. "I hardly think that question is going to ruin your whole season, especially not with the kind of team you guys have."

"I just want things to be the way they were," Lucas said.

"We all want that sometimes," she said.

He went upstairs to write. Not what he didn't know about Gramps, but what he did about Mr. Collins. He didn't think he'd be able to focus on his writing. But he was. For a little while, he did what Gramps was always telling him to do:

Eliminate the noise.

Lucas had spent some time with Mr. Collins the day before, asking him questions about *his* past, about how he came to love reading and writing, what made him want to be a teacher, why teaching English had become his passion.

It was almost bedtime when Lucas closed his laptop. Thought he might leave some time to work on his basketball journal, but he'd do that tomorrow. Maybe he'd have a better idea what to put in there when he knew more about what was going on with Coach Gramps.

But what *was* going on?

Lucas felt as if the more he knew the less he knew.

What he did know was this:

There was a lot going on in his life.

An awful lot.

EIGHTEEN

Lucas tried to explain it all to Maria when it was just the two of them at lunch the next day.

When he finished she said, "You should just drop this now."

"I would have by now," Lucas said, "if that picture hadn't dropped out of the book."

"But it wouldn't have if you hadn't gone up into the attic snooping around," she said.

"I wouldn't call it snooping," Lucas said.

He saw she was smiling at him. Sometimes when she did

that he had to find an excuse to turn away, as if he'd spotted somebody else on the other side of the cafeteria, afraid he might be blushing.

"What would you call it, then?"

"Trying to solve a mystery," he said.

"Maybe it's not that great a mystery," Maria said. "Maybe it's just a story your Gramps doesn't want to tell. You know what I really think you should do?"

"Tell me."

"Tell him you love him next time you see him," she said.

"That's it?" Lucas said.

She smiled again. "My mom says you can never do that enough with the people you love," she said. "And don't you always do what he wants you to do in basketball?"

"Yeah."

"Do that now," she said.

Maria already knew Lucas had picked Mr. Collins to write about now that he wasn't writing about Gramps. Maria had picked her grandmother, because she wanted to write about how inspiring her life had been, starting her own dressmaking business as a young woman. And, she told Lucas, it was more than that. Her grandmother had been born in China. Maria wanted to focus on why her life was such a good example of how immigrants could come to America and lead great

American lives. And she told Lucas that there were things that her grandmother had seen growing up that she didn't like talking about.

"I'm so glad Mr. Collins asked us to do something like this," Maria said.

"Well, I'm not!" Ryan said.

He'd been sitting at another table with some of the other Wolves' players. Now he plopped himself down in the chair next to Maria's.

"Sorry to interrupt," Ryan said.

Maria smiled again. "That's so unlike you."

"I need more help with *my* paper," he said.

"Do you mean you want Lucas to help?" Maria said. "Or both of us?"

"You want to help me too!" he said. "Awesome!"

"Sounds like more of a Lucas thing to me," Maria said.

"Thanks a bunch," Lucas said to her.

"Oh," Maria said, "you don't have to thank me."

"What's the problem now?" Lucas said.

"Other than I can't write?" Ryan said.

"I thought we had you off to a good start," Lucas said.

"But every time I try to write on my own, I get stopped," Ryan said.

He turned to Maria and started to tell her how he couldn't

get less than a B on his paper or he wouldn't be able to finish the basketball season.

"I know," she said.

"You do?" Ryan said

"I think my distant relatives back in China know," Maria said.

Lucas couldn't stop himself from laughing.

"Funny?" Ryan said. "You think this is funny?" He groaned as he put his forehead down on the table.

Maria leaned down close to him and said, "Didn't Mr. Collins tell us that a lot of great writers suffered?"

"I'm not looking for great here," Ryan said. "I'm just looking for doesn't stink."

The bell rang then, ending lunch, and sending them off to their one o'clock class. Lucas told Ryan they could work at his house after they got off the bus, and that he promised to get him unstuck. He was actually looking forward to it, thinking it would take his mind off Gramps. And he was happy to help his friend get through this paper, get a good grade, get on with the basketball season.

He wished he was as confident that things would work out with his grandfather.

More than ever, Lucas wished he could write a happy ending to *that* story.

MIKE LUPICA

He and Ryan worked until it was time for Ryan to leave for dinner. They were up in Lucas's room while his mom was down in the kitchen grading papers of her own. Ryan asked Lucas if his mom might mind terribly just shooting him an A on his paper. Lucas told him he was pretty sure it didn't work that way.

But the work they did was similar to what they'd done the first time they'd worked together. Today Ryan talked about the difference between an individual sport and a team sport, and what it was like being on the court alone. As he did, Lucas took notes. Then he wrote out a few paragraphs as a way of helping Ryan organize his thoughts.

"Now just go home and put this into your own words," Lucas said.

"But they already *are* my words," Ryan said. "We've gone over that already."

Lucas said, "But Mr. Collins talks all the time about how we have to find our own voice. I know you just said this stuff. But when you write it yourself, put it in your voice. Seriously, dude? We're almost there. It's like your shot when we're playing ball. You just have to trust it."

When Ryan was gone, Lucas thought about calling Gramps. But he didn't. Gramps would talk when he was ready. And when he *was* ready, maybe he'd explain everything so that Lucas could understand. Maybe it wasn't as much of a mystery as Lucas thought. Maybe everything would make perfect sense, like when you got to the end of a book. Lucas told himself he had to be patient, even though patience wasn't exactly one of his strong suits.

There was no practice tonight. Dinner probably wouldn't be for another hour or so. He tried to read, but he just couldn't focus. So he put down his book, did the little homework he had to do.

Then he quietly made his way back up to the attic. He wasn't going up there to snoop. He was just curious. He just wanted to know for himself. Even if he found something else, he might show it to his mom, and talk about it with her. But it would just be the two of them. He didn't want to upset Gramps. He didn't want to make him talk about things that he didn't want to talk about. He didn't want this mystery, if it really was one, to come between them.

He just wanted to *know*.

Lucas knew Maria had been right at lunch, and that he should drop this now.

But this time when he went up there, he found the letter.

NINETEEN

Lucas had never paid much attention to his dad's medical books. Without ever asking, he'd always just assumed that his mom kept them because going to med school and becoming a doctor had become his new passion after he'd given up the dream of being a college basketball player.

"He decided that there was a reason he'd gotten hurt," Lucas's mom told him one time. "He was going to help people who'd suffered injuries like his get better."

But for some reason today, he opened the box with some of those books packed in there, trying to imagine his dad having them in his hands, wondering if he could possibly have loved reading them the way he'd loved reading Chip Hilton as a boy. Or the way Lucas loved reading books now.

Lucas smiled as he picked up the book on top, *Orthopaedic Surgery: Principles of Diagnosis and Treatment.* He opened it randomly and read a couple paragraphs and found himself wincing, hoping he never had an injury like the one being described that would have to be diagnosed *or* treated. He picked up another: *Netter's Orthopaedic Clinical Examination.*

The third one was *Textbook of Orthopedic Surgery for Students of Medicine.*

When he opened it, he saw the envelope inside. There was nothing written on the outside of the envelope.

The letter, typewritten, was inside.

Lucas took it over to the desk and sat down, and began to read.

Dear Dad,

This is a letter I might never send. I think of it as my end of a conversation we might never have. I haven't been able to work much lately, because I haven't had the strength. I still have a great attitude. I still keep thinking I can beat this thing. You know how stubborn I am.

Lucas stopped, and smiled, and said out loud, "Wonder where he got it from?"

He kept reading.

You made it pretty clear, my whole life, that you didn't have many happy memories from when you grew up out in California the way you did as a foster child, going from one family to another. And I respected that, even though I told you one time that your history was a part of mine. I remember what you said when I did: "I want you to know me for who I am. Not who I was."

I am stubborn, though. And I've had some time on my hands lately. I know when I've asked about college basketball, you just told me you'd played for a college that wasn't even a college anymore, and even there you hadn't played for long. So I decided to do a little investigating, and see if I could answer some of the questions before . . . well, while I could still ask them.

(Sorry, that didn't sound like my good attitude. Maybe this is just one of those days.)

And then one day I was in Mom's old study. There was this photograph of the two of you, when you were young, and I wanted to have it framed and give it to you for Father's Day. I couldn't find it. But what I did find, in a shoebox in her closet, was a picture of you and another guy in a Bisons jersey, and a date on the back from 1961 that was about the right time for you to be in college. The guys were called "Joe" and "Tommy."

And me, with too much time on his hands now, decided to do a little investigating, thinking I might surprise you with what I found out.

I didn't know that I'd surprise myself instead.

So I know, Dad.

So I know about the Ocean State Bisons. I know about the scandal. I know about Joe Samuels and Tommy Angelo and what you guys did, and why you never wanted to talk about your own basketball career, or about college, or about the life you had in California before you and Mom moved East.

Even as I'm writing this, writing the letter I might never send, full of questions I still don't know if I'll ever ask you to your face about how you came to be Sam Winston, I do realize you were right about something:

Whatever you did and why you did it, I still love
you for who you are.

It doesn't mean I understand why you and your
teammates did what you did. It really is like you
were another person. But it could never change the
dad you've been to me, the husband you were to Mom,
any of that. Maybe I would have felt this way if
I'd found out this stuff when I was a boy. But I
didn't. I'm a man now, still trying to be the man
you always wanted me to be.

I'm not sure why I even kept that picture. Maybe
I should have left it in the box. I'm not positive
why I'm writing this all down. But you know me:
You've always told me I was as full of questions as
I was full of beans.

Lucas stopped again, hearing Gramps telling him at the dinner table last week that he was the one full of beans. He was
starting to tear up, but not because of that.

There was just a little left in the letter.

But if there's one thing I've learned since I
got sick, it's that I know as well as anybody ever
could what really matters. And what matters to me

is the time we've already had together, and the
time we're going to have. (Did I mention that I
don't give up?)

Since I found out what I did, I feel like I've
had a lot of feelings to unpack, all because I had
to unpack that shoebox. But one feeling will never
change:

How much I love you.

Mike

There was a date on the bottom. Lucas looked at it, and realized it was a month before his dad had died.

Now he cried.

TWENTY

The pages that Lucas had printed out, about Joe Samuels and Tommy Angelo and the point-shaving scandal at Ocean State University that had finally put the school out of business, were on the kitchen table. His mom had them in front of her.

She slowly turned page after page, reading the old stories from newspapers that Lucas had already read.

"It's the same as if he lied to us," Lucas said.

"That's not true, honey," she said.

"Well, he didn't tell the truth," Lucas said.

"He just didn't tell us the whole story," she said.

She took off her reading glasses and looked at him across the table.

"I know all this is a shock," she said. "But none of this changes the wonderful man Gramps has been to you."

"You sound like Dad," he said.

"That used to happen a lot," she said.

Lucas reached across and poked a finger on one of the pages in front of his mom.

"No wonder he wanted to be somebody else," Lucas said. "No wonder he turned himself into Sam Winston. He didn't want anybody to know that he tried to fix basketball games when he was in college."

Lucas felt as if he were out of breath.

"When I was online reading about this stuff, you know whose name came up? Clair Bee?"

"He wrote the Chip Hilton books," his mom said.

"They called him *Coach* Clair Bee on some of the covers," Lucas said. "It turned out he'd coached a college team once and this happened with some of his players."

"Your dad told me about it," his mom said. "It was at Long Island University. Coach Bee resigned because of it. But you should know that he also ended up in the Basketball Hall of Fame."

"How can you not think he lied?" Lucas said. "And that means to both of us."

"Maybe he thought the truth would hurt too much," she said.

"Well, at least he got that right," Lucas said.

"But he still has the right to tell us his side of things," she said. "We owe him that."

"Why?" Lucas said.

"Because you love him and he loves you," Julia said.

"I love Sam Winston," Lucas said. "Not Joe Samuels. Not the guy in those stories. Not the *cheater*."

He practically spit out the last word.

"They're the same person," she said in a quiet voice. "Like two sides of the same coin."

"He talks all the time about doing things the right way," Lucas said. "Playing basketball the right way. And now it turns out he did something as wrong in basketball as you could ever do."

He stood up.

"I want to stop talking about this now," he said.

"Okay," she said.

Lucas turned and walked out of the kitchen. He went up to his room and shut the door. He was still angry. He could still feel the heat inside him. And the disappointment. And the shame. But he made himself sit down and open the file on his basketball journal and write about the coach who it turned out he didn't know at all.

When he finished, he shut his laptop and got on his bed.

Then he started to cry again, rolling over so he did it into his pillow, so his mom couldn't hear how much the truth really had hurt him.

TWENTY-ONE

The gym at Claremont Middle was open after school on Friday, so Lucas and Ryan, and Richard and Billy, played two-on-two.

Lucas didn't tell Ryan about Gramps. He hadn't told Maria at lunch, as much as he wanted to, because she was smart and sensible about everything.

For now he just kept what he'd learned from his dad's letter, and then from his own research, to himself.

When they'd lost track of how many games they'd played, Lucas told the guys he was going to stay in the gym and work on some of his stuff alone.

"You want us to find you a sleeping bag so you can sleep here tonight?" Ryan said.

"Just trying to get better," Lucas said.

It was only four thirty. His mom wasn't picking him up until five. Still plenty of gym time left. You never wasted that, even when you were feeling as hurt as Lucas did right now.

So he worked on taking outside shots without dribbling the ball, just catching and shooting, because in a real game, in real time, sometimes you just did the defender a huge favor by taking one more dribble. He worked as hard as ever on his left-handed dribble, working toward his ultimate goal of being as confident going to his left as he was going to his right.

He made himself knock down ten free throws in a row, as usual. So far this season all the work he'd done was paying off, because his free-throw shooting had been pretty solid. He still wanted to be ready when a game was on the line.

He stepped to the line and proceeded to make his first eight.

Then he missed.

He started all over again.

He *was* stubborn, and wasn't ever going to cheat himself.

I'll never cheat the game.

He got to nine in a row.

Missed the tenth, feeling like a choker.

Started all over again.

He looked at the clock as he did. Five minutes to five. But he pretended it was a game clock. Told himself he wasn't trying to make ten in a row in the next five minutes.

Told himself that every shot he knocked down *was* with a game on the line.

He got to nine again.

Lucas went through his routine. Took one last look at the rim after one last bounce of the ball. Took a deep breath.

Knocked it down like a champ.

"Ten for ten," the voice behind him said.

He didn't have to turn around to know it was Gramps.

He was limping in Lucas's direction from the other end of the court. He wore his faded black Celtics cap with the shamrock on the front.

He walked all the way to where Lucas stood at the free-throw line, ball on his hip.

"I let your mother know I'd pick you up and give you a ride home when she told me where you were," he said. "Told her we needed to talk. All of us need to talk, now that I think about it. But first you and me."

"Mom told you that we know about you?" Lucas said.

"She did," Gramps said. "And you do know. Just not all of it."

"You lied to me!" Lucas said, unable to control himself. "Everything I thought is a big fat lie!"

"No, son, it's not," Gramps said.

Even trying to keep his voice low, it sounded loud in the empty gym. Just not as loud as Lucas's had been.

"I don't even know you!" Lucas yelled.

He could never remember raising his voice to his grandfather, not one time. But he'd never had a reason, until now.

"You do know me," Gramps said. "Just not who I used to be. Even if that dumb boy made me the man I am now."

"You took money to cheat the game," Lucas said.

"The person I really cheated was myself," he said. "Now come sit down so we can have a talk we should have had a long time ago."

There were two folding chairs set up at one of the corners of the court. Gramps walked toward them. Lucas followed.

"I'm not going to make excuses for what I did," he said. "But I'd rather you heard the whole story from me instead of reading it."

They both sat down. Gramps talked for a long time then.

Ocean State had been a pretty famous program in college basketball, starting in the 1930s, and had nearly made a Final Four during World War II. He'd gotten a scholarship there from Bakersfield High School. The Ocean State program hadn't been great for a long time, but Joe Samuels decided he could be one of the guys who could restore its former glory.

"The tournament was a lot smaller in those days," he said. "I thought we had a chance. This was before UCLA got great and started winning almost every year."

Lucas just listened.

"It wasn't just me who was a dumb kid," Gramps said. "We were all dumb kids, most of us lucky to have a scholarship, because just about every one of us on the team came from almost no money at all."

He didn't even know his teammates were taking money at first. But slowly he started to wonder about some things he was seeing, especially at the end of games. Tommy Angelo would start throwing the ball away, and big leads would become small leads. There were a couple games that they shouldn't have come close to losing, but nearly did. The two guys messing up the most were Tommy Angelo and the team's center, Ed Dolph.

Finally one day Gramps asked Tommy Angelo why he seemed to turn into a different player in the last five minutes.

Tommy was from Las Vegas. He had uncles who worked in the casino business. He took Gramps out for a burger one night and explained that a couple friends of the family had shot some money his way and asked him to "manipulate" the point spread in certain games.

"That's the big word he used for trying to do the same as fix a fight," Gramps said. "Manipulate."

Now Lucas spoke.

"Why didn't you tell the coach?" he said.

"I told him I was going to," Gramps said. "But Tommy said that Coach was in on it and that there were only five or six games left in the season and they could all make some extra money and never do it again.

"No harm, no foul, he said," Gramps told Lucas.

Gramps told Tommy Angelo he'd rather quit playing basketball than do that. Tommy said that if he ever told anybody, Tommy would tell the whole world that Gramps had been in on it too.

That same night, someone threw a brick through the front window of the grocery store that Gramps's parents owned back in Bakersfield. It was, he said, the same as a threat.

"It was a message," he said. "I had to go along to get along." He gave Lucas a long look. "And so I did."

Until the whole thing blew up on all of them.

Somehow a reporter from the *Los Angeles Times* got a tip about what was going on with the Ocean State Bisons. The tip turned into a source in Las Vegas. The reporter went back and looked at the games that had been "manipulated." He went back to Las Vegas and did some checking and found out that a lot of money had been bet on Ocean State in those games, way more than the usual amount.

"It wasn't every game," Gramps said to Lucas.

"Is that supposed to make it all better?" Lucas said.

"I was dumb and scared," Gramps said. "That's a reason, I know, and not an excuse. I wasn't just afraid for me, I was afraid for my family."

"You told me once that character was doing the right thing even if no one is around to see," Lucas said.

"I know I did," Gramps said. "I know."

He went on with his story.

Maybe if Ocean State had been some big basketball powerhouse at the time, it would have been an even bigger story. It was still big enough that the story made news all over the country. The four players involved, included Joe Samuels, were arrested one day at the gym right before practice.

"Even that suspended sentence felt like jail," Gramps said, "just without being in jail."

They were all expelled from Ocean State on the spot.

"What did your foster parents do?" Lucas said.

"They took me in when I came back home," Gramps said. "It's what parents do, even after you break their hearts."

But they closed their grocery store about six months later. It was because of the shame they felt in front of their friends and customers, Gramps said. They ended up moving to Vancouver, in Canada, thinking that no one would know them, or care about what Joe Samuels had done.

Gramps didn't go with them.

"What did you do?" Lucas said.

"Getting to that," Gramps said.

"First tell me how you became Sam Winston," Lucas said.

He wanted to know all of it now. There was no going back, for either one of them.

"I legally changed my name," he said. "It's not as hard to do as you might think. After I did, I worked odd jobs here and there. Worked for the railroad. Worked at a radio station. Worked some construction. Then finally I joined the army, even shipped out and spent some in the war in Vietnam."

"You fought in a war?" Lucas said.

Gramps nodded.

"I guess that's just one more thing about you I didn't know," he said.

"Even got shot right above the knee one time for my trouble," he said. "My other knee just wore down over time from favoring the one that got shot."

He was discharged from the army after that. He came back to California and got a job as a carpenter. He said he'd always been good with his hands. He met a young woman and fell in love and got married.

"Did Grandmom know what you'd done?" Lucas said. "Did she know who you really were?"

"She knew every bit of it," Gramps said. "I told her one night just like I told you."

They finally decided to move to the other side of the country. If they were going to start a new life together, they might as well make it a really new life. He'd changed his name. He'd gotten married. He thought of Claremont as a new beginning.

"I decided," he said, "to live a life and not an apology."

He went to work for the post office. He became a dad. He got into coaching, he said, because of his son, who loved all sports, but basketball most of all. When people would ask him about his life before Claremont, he was vague enough with his answers that people finally gave up asking the questions.

"They just came to know me for who I was," Gramps said.

Lucas knew it was getting late. He knew Gramps had been talking for a long time. But he wasn't ready to leave yet.

And there was still a big question he wanted to ask.

"How did Dad find out?" Lucas said.

His grandfather pulled his hat off his head and ran an old hand through his short white hair. Then he put his hat back on.

"That's the thing," he said. "I didn't know that he had, until now. I didn't know that I'd already let him down before I let you down."

"You never saw that letter?" Lucas said.

Gramps shook his head.

"So he never asked you about any of it?" Lucas said.

"He died," Gramps said.

Lucas looked down and realized he'd been holding his basketball in his lap the whole time Gramps had been talking. He could feel himself squeezing both sides of it now, as if trying to squeeze the air right out of it.

He was feeling himself breathing hard. Even though it had been Gramps telling the story, it was Lucas who felt worn out by it.

"I'm sorry," Gramps said.

"Not as sorry as I am," Lucas said.

"I'm not asking you to forgive me," he said, "or even understand why I did what I did. I'm still not sure why I did everything I did. Or didn't do what I know I should have done at the time. I haven't told you all of it tonight. But I didn't leave out anything important."

All because of a school paper, Lucas thought.

He looked at his grandfather, slumped now in his chair, looking older than he ever had before, like the oldest man on Earth.

"At least now it's out in the open," Gramps said. "And I'm not making excuses for what I did. The things that happened, I *let* them happen."

"What about the money?" Lucas said.

He had meant to ask about the money before. The stories he'd printed out said Joe Samuels had been paid five thousand dollars, and that Tommy Angelo had gotten more.

"I kept it in a pocket of a jacket hanging in the closet of my dorm room," Gramps said. "I thought that when the school year was over I could take it home and give it to my parents and tell them I'd gotten a job when I wasn't playing basketball."

Lucas shook his head quickly now, from side to side, feeling the anger rising up in him again.

"You should have been brave enough to tell," Lucas said.

"You don't think I know that?" Gramps said in a tired voice.

"I want to go home now," Lucas said.

He stood up and bounced the ball as hard as he could, then caught it, and bounced it again, even harder than before. The sound of the ball hitting the floor was very loud.

"Are you sure you haven't told me more lies?" Lucas said.

"Everything I've told you is the truth, son," Gramps said.

"It's like you lied to me my whole life!" Lucas said.

"Until now," Gramps said.

"Until you got caught again," Lucas said.

Gramps stared at him. Lucas saw the hurt in his eyes. Then his grandfather said, "The worst part of all this wasn't that everybody ended up knowing what I'd done. The worst part was that I knew."

He started walking toward the doors at the other end of the gym. Gramps followed him. His whole life his grandfather had tried to be like his father, too. He'd coached Lucas the way he'd coached Lucas's own father. All he'd ever wanted was to be in a gym like this with him. All he'd wanted to do was learn basketball from him and talk basketball with him. Gramps had been the only coach he'd ever wanted. Or needed. He'd even dreamed that Gramps would somehow get to coach him at Claremont High.

Now he wasn't sure that he even wanted him to be his coach tomorrow.

Or ever again.

TWENTY-TWO

But Gramps did coach the Wolves on Saturday.

Lucas tried to act as if things were normal between him and Gramps. But once they were back in the gym together, Lucas managed to stay away from him as much as possible. He just wanted to concentrate on basketball today.

Then the game started and it was as if he'd forgotten how to play basketball. Or at least winning basketball. Or play smart basketball.

He couldn't make a shot. He felt like he had more turnovers in the first quarter of this one game than all the other games he'd played this season combined. He got caught in switches on defense. Sometimes he just got beat at that end of the court. His teammates seemed to be working around him today, and not with him.

By the end of the quarter Lucas kept sneaking looks at his grandfather, waiting for him to take him out. But when Lucas threw another pass away early in the second quarter, with the Wolves in the lead despite him, he did something he'd never done before in his life.

He called a time-out and took him*self* out of the game.

"You need to put Neil in for me," Lucas said. "He'll give us a better chance. I can't do anything."

"I'm still the coach of this team," Gramps said when Lucas got to the bench, keeping his voice low, maybe as a way of trying to calm down Lucas, even though *that* wasn't about to happen.

"Then start acting like one," Lucas said.

Now Gramps told him to go sit down. Lucas did, as far away from his grandfather as possible. When he got there, he turned and looked out at the court. Ryan was staring at him, almost like he was staring at a stranger.

But that's what Lucas felt like to himself today.

He didn't play great in the second half. But at least he'd stopped embarrassing himself. Jake Farr was still having a better game at point for the Mavs than Lucas was for the Wolves. A *much* better game. But Jake was no longer dominating Lucas when he had the ball. And Lucas, even though he still couldn't find his shot, had stopped turning the ball over. He had started distributing the ball to his teammates and making better decisions.

There was a point early in the fourth quarter when the game started to get away, and the Wolves managed to waste a ten-point lead. But Gramps kept Lucas out there. Ryan hit a couple of huge shots in the last two minutes. The Wolves ended up winning by four. They stayed unbeaten.

Ryan waited until they were all finished with the handshake line until he pulled Lucas aside.

"Okay, what happened out there?" Ryan said, whispering just loud enough for Lucas to hear.

"Bad day," Lucas said.

"Dude," Ryan said, "you took yourself out of a game. I didn't think you'd do that even if you had a broken leg."

"Hey, we won," Lucas said.

Ryan was staring at him, frowning. "Did something happen?"

"I'm good," Lucas said.

"Don't lie to me," Ryan said.

"Everybody lies once in a while," Lucas said.

"Now what is *that* supposed to mean?" Ryan said. "You never lie."

"It doesn't mean anything," Lucas said. "Like I said. Just a bad day."

Usually after games, Lucas would try to find time to break down what had happened with Gramps, both the good and bad. But he knew that wasn't happening today. He already knew what had happened. He'd been distracted, and let that affect his play, and nearly cost his team a game. Unacceptable. Maybe, because the Wolves had managed to hang on to their lead in the end, everything looked pretty much the same as always if you were watching from the stands.

But Lucas knew that everything was different, and that maybe nothing was ever going to be the same for him again.

Gramps had already left the gym. Some of the guys were talking about going to Gus's for pizza. Ryan asked Lucas if he wanted to join them. Lucas said he'd pass, he had some school-work to do. And the way he'd played today, he'd probably drop his slice on the floor when he went to eat it.

"Schoolwork?" Ryan said. "On a Saturday? After we won a game? Dude, now I know you're having some kind of melt."

"Crazy, right?" Lucas said.

He told Ryan that maybe he'd call him later, and they could hang out. He promised his attitude would be better by then. Ryan said he was holding him to that.

"I hate playing lousy," Lucas said. "Usually going up against somebody like Jake brings out the best in me. Not today."

"You never play lousy," Ryan said. "Sometimes you just don't play great."

"But I want to, every single time."

"Even LeBron has bad games," Ryan said. "Heck, his first year with the Lakers, he had a bad *season*."

Lucas managed a grin.

"So you're admitting I played bad," he said.

"I give up," Ryan said. "Sometimes I can't win with you."

In the car on the way home Lucas's mom said, "We'll have to find a way to fix this. With you and Gramps, I mean."

"I'm not sure it can be fixed," Lucas said. "I know he says he's sorry. But aren't you the one who says that sorry doesn't fix the lamp?"

"The love between the two of you just didn't go away because you found that picture and that letter your dad wrote," she said.

"Not saying I'm gonna stop loving him," Lucas said. "But I can't help it if I don't trust him anymore."

They were at a light. She turned to look at him.

"Honey," she said. "He made a bad mistake. But people make mistakes, especially when they're young. That doesn't define who they are. From everything I know, your grandfather made a conscious decision not to let his mistake define who he is. He got knocked down and picked himself back up and tried to make something of himself. And by the way? He became someone I know you admire as much as anybody you've ever met."

"Used to admire," Lucas said.

The light changed. They were just a couple blocks from home.

"Eventually you're not going to be as angry as you are now," she said.

"Can I hold you to that?" Lucas said.

Now his mom was making the turn on to their street.

"This whole thing has hurt him enough," Julia said. "You don't want to be the one who hurts him more."

"What about the way I'm hurting?" Lucas said.

"It will get better," she said.

"I hold you to that, too," Lucas said to his mom.

He just knew it wasn't getting better today. He tried to remember a time when he'd ever felt anything like this after winning a game.

But he couldn't.

TWENTY-THREE

Lucas didn't call Ryan and ask him to hang out. He actually did do some schoolwork on a Saturday. He wanted to finish his English paper before the deadline. There was enough going on his life right now. He didn't need one more distraction.

So he stayed at it until it was time for dinner. When it was just him and his mom at the table, he talked about his writing. Not basketball. Not today's game.

Not Gramps.

For a change.

• • •

The next morning, after Lucas's mom had treated him to a pancake breakfast at the Claremont Diner, Gramps was waiting for them when they got home, sitting on the front porch.

When he stood, Lucas's mom immediately gave him a hug.

"Sam Winston," she said, as if lecturing a child. "You know you have a key to this house. You didn't have to sit out here in the cold."

"Couldn't find the darn thing," he said. "Getting worse and worse finding keys the older I get. And not just keys."

He looked at both of them then and said, "I won't be here long. I just need to talk to Lucas."

They went inside. Lucas's mom asked Gramps if he wanted some hot chocolate, one of his favorites. He said no thanks. They all took seats in the living room. Lucas and his mom sat next to each other on the couch. Gramps turned around the chair from which he usually watched basketball, so he was facing both of them.

"Let me get right to it," he said. "I gave some thought, in light of everything, to quitting the team and letting Ryan's mom finish out the season. Or letting them see if they wanted to hire somebody else, if she couldn't coach full-time."

He sighed.

"But then when I thought about it a little more, I decided

that there's no one in this town better than me at coaching these boys," he said. "I may be a lot of things. But a quitter sure isn't one of them."

"Okay," Lucas said.

"Wasn't asking for your okay," Gramps said.

Lucas started to say something, but his grandfather held up a hand to stop him.

"I love you as much as I ever did, son, even knowing I let you down," he said. "I love you even knowing that things have changed between us and might not ever change back. It's because of things I did that I can't go back and fix, and that's on me. But what I'm not here to do is ask your permission to coach the Wolves."

Suddenly Lucas felt himself getting angry all over again.

"I never said you needed my permission," Lucas said. "That's not what this is about, and you know it."

"Then what is it about?" Gramps said.

"It's about you!" Lucas said. He wasn't shouting. But he was close. "Not only did you cheat, you hid what you did from Mom and me. And you thought you were hiding it from Dad when he was still alive."

Lucas saw Gramps's face redden. He'd never seen his grandfather angry. But he looked angry now. They both had things they wanted to get off their chest today, neither one of them willing to give an inch, like they were fighting for a loose ball.

It was Gramps who backed down first.

"You know something?" he said. "You're right. Hiding it was wrong. And I can see why you think that's even worse than what I did when I was in college. Because hiding it just made things worse."

"A lot worse," Lucas said.

"But now we've got to figure this out, you and me," Gramps said. "As good a player as you are and as good a teammate as we both know you are, you let your feelings about me get in the way of what was best for your team today." He paused, but only for a second. "Do you understand what I'm telling you? That if I'm still going to be the coach, I'm the one who has to be in charge?"

"I do understand," Lucas said.

"And you're good with that?"

"Yes."

"Is that the truth?"

"*I* tell the truth," Lucas said.

"Lucas," his mom said. "Please watch your tone. I know there's a lot going on here. But he's still your grandfather."

"It's fine, Julia," Gramps said. "Boy's got a right to blow off some steam." He turned back to Lucas. "But I don't want you to ever call a time-out like that and take yourself out of a game ever again. Is *that* understood?"

"It is," Lucas said.

"If you don't show me respect," Gramps said, "the others won't. They take their lead from you."

"They don't know what you did," Lucas said.

"No, son, they don't," Gramps said. "Those other boys don't know. And if you choose to tell them about me, well, that's up to you, nothing I can do to stop you. But if there's one thing I still know, it's how I want players to play and how I want them to act, and not just when they're having a good day."

Lucas took in some air, a lot of it, like he was blowing off some steam. There was more that he wanted to say to him now, a lot more, put it all out there once and for all, let Gramps know how angry he was, and hurt, and betrayed. But in that moment, he didn't want to make things worse than they already were. They were already bad enough.

And he was smart enough to know that Gramps was right about the way Lucas had acted today.

"It won't happen again," Lucas said.

His grandfather pushed down with a hand on each knee, as a way of getting himself out of his chair. This time it took him two tries, but he finally made it.

"I'll see you tomorrow night at practice," Gramps said.

Julia said, "I'm glad you came by, Sam."

"I can see myself out," he said.

When Gramps was gone, Lucas's mom turned to him and said, "Now I want to say something."

"Mom, I got the message," Lucas said. "I did."

"That was his message, not mine," she said. "Would you like to hear it?"

Lucas smiled and said, "Do I have a choice?"

"Never," she said.

She smiled.

"You only get so many seasons in your life," Lucas's mom said. "Not all of them are going to be special. This one still has a chance to be."

"I know that," Lucas said.

"I know you know," she said. "You're not just a smart basketball boy. You're smart, period. So the choice you have to make is whether you're going to make the most of this season going forward. Because if you don't, you'll always regret it. I asked your dad one time, after he got sick, if he had any regrets. He smiled at me—he had a great smile, your dad—and said, "Other than not still being a kid?"

"You think Dad really did forgive Gramps, even if he never got to tell him?" Lucas said.

"It never would have occurred to your dad *not* to forgive him," she said.

"You don't know that."

"But I knew him," she said. "And he knew better than any-body not to waste energy or a day of his life on things that he couldn't change, on anything that didn't matter. It was all there in the letter."

He thought she might cry. She did sometimes when she was talking about his dad. Instead she broke into an even bigger smile than before.

"Now get outside and shoot some hoops in the driveway," she said.

It was exactly what Lucas did. He knew this wasn't the season he'd expected. It wasn't the season he wanted it to be, for him or for Gramps. There were things *he* couldn't change.

But the season still mattered.

A lot.

And it really was the only one he had.

TWENTY-FOUR

Practices before next Saturday's game against the Oakdale Owls was different for Lucas. Not bad. Not even weird. Just different.

Gramps was acting as if things were back to normal with Lucas after what had happened in the last game. He wasn't treating Lucas any differently than the rest of the Wolves. He had put in a new zone press for the Oakdale Owls. He drew up some plays that took Ryan away from his usual forward position and put him in the backcourt with Lucas, saying he thought that move might create real matchup problems for the other team.

"Christmas is right around the corner," Gramps said. "Maybe in the right moment, we'll treat a big guard like Ryan as a brand-new toy."

"Like I'm a video game, Mr. Winston?" Ryan said.

"Yeah," Richard said. "Ryan 2K."

If you didn't know that Gramps and Lucas were related, you wouldn't have been able to tell by the way they acted around each other on the court. Lucas was still playing ball *with* his buddies, and *for* his grandfather. He still loved being out there, loved the process of practice, of learning things on offense and defense. He loved the process of getting better. But he knew things weren't the way they'd always been, could see that they weren't, even if his teammates couldn't. Gramps would still pull him aside and tell him there might have been a better way to run a play. He'd still give Lucas a shout-out when he made a particularly good move.

It was just different, no getting around it. Gramps was still right there, limping out to the middle of the court when he wanted to make a point, still teaching. But it was as if there was distance between them.

And Gramps, at least for now, had stopped coming over to the house for dinner. Lucas wanted to talk with Ryan or Maria about what was really going on. But he couldn't do that without telling them who Gramps really was, and what he'd done.

So the only person to talk about it with was his mom, though Lucas was starting to worry that she must feel she was having the same conversation with him, over and over and over again.

"When is this going to get better?" Lucas said. "You keep telling me this is going to get better."

He told her about the feeling he had that there was this big distance now between him and Gramps.

"Maybe not until the season is over," she said. "And the two of you can put some real distance between yourselves. Maybe then you can find your way back to each other."

It was the night before the Owls game, to be played at the Oakdale YMCA. Lucas's mom had cooked up homemade pizza for them. He didn't know how she did it, but her pizza tasted even better to him than Gus's, not that he would ever tell Gus something like that.

"Or maybe it won't ever get any better than it is right now," Lucas's mom added. "Maybe this is what people like to call a new normal."

"Doesn't feel normal to me," he said.

"Or me," she said.

"I hate this," Lucas said.

"Just remember that you don't hate him," Julia said.

"I can still hate what he did," Lucas said.

"There's a difference," she said. "And a distinction."

"I just don't see either one sometimes," he said.

She tented her fingers and put them under her chin and smiled at him.

"You are a spectacular twelve-year-old boy," she said, "as prejudiced as I might be on this particular subject. But I have to remind myself sometimes that you are still twelve years old."

Lucas was already working on his third piece of pizza. He noticed his mom was still working on her first. He had never understood how she could control herself like that.

"What does that mean?" Lucas said.

"It means that just because you're not ready to forgive your grandfather now, one of these days you're going to be," she said.

"For what he and his teammates did?" Lucas said. "Or for him pretending to be somebody he wasn't my whole life?"

"But that's the thing," she said. "He hasn't been pretending. Gramps is who he is. He's the sum of everything that ever happened to him, the way we all are, whether he shared all of it with us or not."

"I'm gonna get another slice," he said. "Okay?"

"I'd be insulted if you didn't," his mom said.

He got one from the counter and sat back down.

"But if Gramps was the person I always thought he was," he said, "he wouldn't have been able to cheat the game like he did."

"People change," she said.

"You never do."

"Everybody changes, honey. You change, your life changes. Look at mine. Your dad and me were going to live happily ever after."

Just like that, a sad look came across her face, a shadow that appeared out of nowhere, and her smile was gone. It happened that way sometimes, even when she was sharing a happy memory about his dad. Lucas knew what a happy, positive person his mom was. But maybe she was right, what she'd just said about Gramps. Maybe everybody was the sum of everything that had ever happened to them. Good or bad.

He didn't know what to say. She had told him once that you could never go wrong keeping your mouth shut when you didn't have anything to say.

"Only the 'ever after' for the two of us became the two of *us*," she said. "You and me."

"I'm sorry I keep bringing this up," Lucas said. "We start out talking about Gramps and then we end up talking about Dad."

She took her right hand now and placed it on the table between them, palms up. Lucas put his hand inside it. As always, it fit like a glove.

"I've been telling you this in different ways your whole life," she said. "All of us just have to remember how precious every

MIKE LUPICA

day is. And not waste time trying to change things we can't."

"Like what?" Lucas said.

"Like the past," she said. "Yours. Gramps's. Mine. Everybody's."

"Mom," he said. "I hear you. I know what you're saying. But I know I'm still mad."

She gave his hand a squeeze.

"Maybe that anger will end up in the past someday," she said, "even if it doesn't change the way you feel right now."

When they were done cleaning the kitchen together, he went into the living room to watch the Celtics play the Bucks. He loved the kind of team ball the Celtics played. Gramps had always told him it was part of the Celtics tradition, in their own way-back machine, that they'd practically invented team ball in the NBA back in the fifties and sixties when they used to win the championship almost every year.

Funny, he thought.

Even when he was angry, and disappointed, and ashamed of what Gramps had done, he'd hear something inside his head that Gramps had said.

He loved talking about the way-back machine in basketball.

Just not, as it turned out, when the conversation was about him.

TWENTY-FIVE

I t was about a half-hour's drive from Claremont to Oakdale. Lucas had heard his mom talking to Gramps on her phone after breakfast, telling him that they could all drive together.

But then he heard her say, "Are you sure? We'd love to have the company."

Lucas heard her inviting him to dinner, then heard a slight pause.

"Okay," she said. "But if you change your mind, you know it's no problem for me to set an extra place."

When Lucas walked into the kitchen she said, "I guess you heard?"

"I did."

She shook her head. "The new normal."

"It must be the normal he wants," Lucas said.

"I don't think any of us wants this," she said.

The game against the Owls was a lot like their first game of the season: They dug a big hole for themselves early. They were playing solid defense, but not solid enough, as it turned out. The Owls just couldn't miss. Most of the scoring damage was being done by their two guards, Gary Cullen and Len Shenfeld. They were both big, they could both shoot, they could both handle the ball. If you were just watching the game from the stands in the Oakdale Y, you would have had a hard time deciding which one was the point guard and which one was the shooting guard. It made Lucas remember something else Gramps liked to talk about when he got into his way-back machine:

They were both just guards. Not point guards. Not shooting guards.

Just guards.

During every time-out in the first half, as the Wolves couldn't dent the Owls' fourteen-point lead, Gramps would say the same thing:

"We're fine."

Lucas didn't think they were. Their zone press hadn't worked this time. Gary Cullen and Len Shenfeld were just too good with the ball. Even when the Wolves would have one of them trapped in the backcourt, they would find a way to make a pass over the top of the defense, and the Owls would end up with another easy basket.

They were the ones playing basketball the right way today.

A lot righter than us, Lucas thought.

Their lead was still twelve halfway through the third quarter. The Wolves were shooting a little better by then, the Owls shooting a little worse. But Lucas knew that if something didn't change, and soon, the Wolves were about to lose their first game of the season.

Maybe it was just one of those days. Maybe the other team was just better today, no matter how much the Wolves tried to change things up.

Only Lucas just wasn't ready to concede that.

At the end of a time-out the Owls had called, Lucas said to Gramps, "We should try what we worked on in practice the other night."

"We worked on a lot of things," Gramps said.

The other Wolves players in the game were already walking back on the court. It was just Lucas and Gramps. Talking basketball. Trying to figure it out.

For now, things were the way they used to be.

"How about we put Ryan in the backcourt?" Lucas said. "Let him bring the ball up. Make Len match up with him instead of trying to have Sharif and Neil match up with Len."

Gramps nodded.

"Maybe I should have thought of that myself."

"You did," Lucas said.

"Think it will work?"

"All we've got to lose is the game," Lucas said.

The ref blew his whistle.

"That's a lot to lose," Gramps said.

"I know," Lucas said.

"Go make it happen."

"I'll try," Lucas said.

"Everybody tries," Gramps said.

Ryan took the ball from the ref, ready to inbound it to Lucas. Only Lucas took the ball, and quickly whispered the plan to his best friend.

"Trust me," Lucas said.

"Always," Ryan said.

"Let's win the game," Lucas said.

They didn't run pick-and-rolls now. Instead the Wolves spread the court, giving Ryan plenty of room to operate. He wasn't waiting for Lucas to throw him the ball now. He had the ball. First time down, he blew past the kid who had been guarding him, Juanell Robinson, for an easy layup. The Owls lead was ten. Gary missed an open shot. This time, as Ryan was bringing the ball up, Len switched over to guard him. Lucas took a step out on the wing, as if coming to the ball, but then stopped and broke for the basket. Ryan hit him with a pass. Lucas got a layup.

Now the lead was eight.

It hadn't even taken a minute. But the Owls looked rattled now. Sometimes it didn't take much. Ryan pressured Len as he brought the ball up, swallowing him up with all his length. Len got rid of the ball too quickly and Lucas was sitting on the crosscourt pass Len tried to throw to Gary. He picked it off cleanly, streaked down the court alone, laid the ball in.

Now it was 38–32, Owls.

Len missed now, forcing a shot. Billy got the rebound, snapped off an outlet pass to Ryan, who took the ball to the middle and led the fast break. Lucas was to his left. When Len came up on Ryan, trying to force him to pass, Ryan *did* pass, to Lucas, streaking again for the basket. He caught the pass in stride, confidently put the ball on the floor with his left hand—all the extra work he'd done with his left hand paying off—laid the ball off the backboard with his left hand, getting fouled by Gary in the process.

He went to the line. It wasn't late in a game. It wasn't the last minute. But he felt as if this was the first big free throw of the season for him, a chance to make it a one-possession game if the Wolves could get another stop and make a three-pointer.

Lucas went through his routine. Took a deep breath. Even visualized the ball going through the basket the way Gramps had taught him. Made the free throw.

They were down three.

Same two teams on the court. But it was a different game.

The Wolves and Owls were tied going into the fourth quarter. Gramps kept moving guys in and out. He gave Lucas a one-minute breather at the start of the fourth. He did the same with Ryan a minute after that, not wanting to have both of them out of the game at the same time, even for a few seconds.

With four minutes to go, it was the Wolves who were ahead by five points. They were the ones who couldn't miss now. Lucas and Ryan were the ones handling the Owls' press with ease.

Lucas remembered one time when Mike Breen, his favorite announcer in the NBA, said that when momentum changed in a game, it was like trying to turn an ocean liner around. That's what happened at the Oakdale YMCA in the second half.

Different backcourt for the Wolves, different game.

Only one thing hadn't changed for the Wolves by the time the horn sounded:

They were still undefeated.

TWENTY-SIX

It was the last full week of school before Christmas break began the following Wednesday. The Wolves had won two more games by then, and suddenly there were just three more games left before the top two teams in their league would play for the championship. And if the Wolves could win the championship, they'd qualify for the state tournament for seventh-grade All-Star and travel teams.

If Lucas had been asked to describe his relationship with Gramps lately, he thought this was the word he would use:

Polite.

It was the best he could do.

Neither of them had mentioned the Ocean State Bisons again. They'd had no disagreements, on or off the court. Maybe it had something to do with the Wolves playing as well as they were, and neither one of them wanted to do anything that might get in the way of that, or hurt the team.

One night at practice, Gramps had been talking to the team about decisions a coach has to make, during a game and during a season, and had said, "You don't always have to like what you do. Sometimes your players *hate* what you're doing. But if it's for the good of the team, you have to do it."

So they were polite with each other, as if they sensed that was what was best for the Wolves. There was still all this distance between them. Lucas realized he'd stopped feeling angry about who Gramps was and what he'd done all the time. But he also realized that the anger wasn't ever very far away. And probably wasn't ever going away.

Their next practice was on Tuesday night. On Monday, Mr. Collins told Lucas and Ryan he wanted to see them after class. He wasn't smiling, or acting like friendly Mr. C., when he said it.

"That doesn't sound good," Ryan said to Lucas when English class ended.

It wasn't.

They had passed in their papers the previous Friday along with everybody else in the class. Lucas had asked Ryan if he wanted him to look over Ryan's paper one more time. Ryan said, no, it was as good as it was going to get.

His mom had once told him something an old writer had said, about how she hated to write but loved having written. But it didn't work that way with Lucas. It would have been like saying that he loved winning a game but not having had to actually play it.

Writing wasn't always easy. It was hard some nights, especially when he was still working on his basketball journal, and had to be honest about everything that had happened since the start of the Wolves' season. Mr. C. was right, though. The more you worked at it, the better you got.

Now Lucas and Ryan sat in the front of Mr. C.'s classroom. He was at his desk. In front of him were two printouts, side by side. He still wasn't smiling, or acting friendly. Clearly there was something bothering him.

He tapped one printout, then the other, then looked up at Lucas and Ryan.

"I've got both your papers here," Mr. Collins said. "Yours, Lucas. And yours, Ryan."

He paused, but they both could see that he wasn't finished.

And seemed even less happy than when they'd arrived.

"There's a problem, I'm sorry to say," he said. "A big problem."

He blew out some air, sounding tired.

"The writing in them is too much alike," he said. "As if they were both written by the same person."

Now he looked directly at Lucas.

"As a matter of fact, they both read as if they were written by you, Lucas."

Lucas cleared his throat, which suddenly felt as dry as the papers on the desk. But before he could speak, Mr. Collins did.

"Every writer has their own voice," he said. "You've both heard me say that plenty of times in class. A writer's voice, even now, can be as distinctive as your handwriting. Or even the way you shoot a basketball. But it's their own. And needs to be their own."

Lucas looked over at Ryan, whose eyes were pleading with him, though he wasn't quite sure pleading for what. Maybe not to make things worse.

He was pretty certain he knew what had happened, that Ryan hadn't changed what Lucas had written, that he'd just left it exactly the way it was. But Lucas felt that if he tried to explain that to Mr. Collins, he *would* make things worse.

Especially for Ryan.

"I was just trying to help Ryan out," Lucas said. "I knew how important it was for him to get a good grade, so he wouldn't get kicked off the basketball team."

"Kicked off the team?" Mr. Collins said. "By your grandfather, Lucas? That doesn't sound like the Gramps I know."

Little do you know, Lucas thought.

Ryan jumped in now.

"I can't get anything less than a B this semester," Ryan said. "I think I'm okay in my other classes. But you said these papers are going to make up most of our grade in English. And I just flat-out stink at writing, even though I know you'd never say that."

He cleared his throat.

"Anyway," Ryan said, "if I get a C, I can't play sports second semester. My mom was a serious basketball player. But she's just as serious about school. And my dad is more serious than her."

Mr. Collins held up one of the papers.

"That's all well and good," he said. "But it's clear that this isn't your work. It's Lucas's."

He turned to Lucas again.

"Did you write this paper for Ryan so he could stay on the basketball team?" Mr. Collins said. "Because if you did, it's not just Ryan who cheated. You both did."

Lucas knew he hadn't cheated. He knew he was just trying to help Ryan out. Get him started. He'd trusted Ryan to go home and take the words he'd spoken to Lucas and then write them out himself. In his own voice. That was all. Lucas knew he'd never cheated in anything in his life. He'd never copy off somebody else's paper or let anybody copy his. It wasn't who he was.

He *hated* any kind of cheating, even when it had involved someone he loved.

Somehow, though, he still felt caught. Ryan wasn't just his teammate. He was Lucas's best friend. The last thing Lucas wanted to do was get him—or them—in more trouble.

"I was just trying to help," Lucas said.

He wasn't going to lie. But he didn't know how he could help things by telling the whole story.

"Lucas knows what a bad writer I am," Ryan said.

"You're not a bad writer," Mr. Collins said. "You just don't love it. And let's be honest, you don't work nearly hard enough at it."

"I guess I tried a little too hard," Lucas said.

"In the process," Mr. Collins said, "it appears that your work became Ryan's."

They all sat there in silence. Lucas felt his brain spinning, as if there were a hundred thoughts inside it at once. Everything that had happened, and was happening, with Gramps had started *because* of this paper. He'd wanted Gramps to be his subject. Gramps had said no. Then he'd found out who Gramps really was, found out Gramps had been part of a cheating scandal that involved his college basketball team, even though he was still saying he hadn't actually cheated himself.

Now here he sat in front of Mr. Collins, who *had* become the subject of his paper, in trouble because of somebody else's paper.

He didn't just feel dizzy. He felt a little bit sick.

"I'm not a cheater," Lucas said.

"I'm not either," Ryan said.

Mr. Collins got up and came around his desk. He placed Ryan's paper on the desk in front of him.

"Maybe neither one of you thought you were doing anything wrong," he said. "Or thought you were being dishonest. I understand the pressure you're obviously feeling about your grade, Ryan. I do. It's why I'm going to give you a second chance."

"You're not going to fail me?" Ryan said.

Lucas could never remember seeing his friend as scared as he was right now. Not in sports. Not anywhere. He watched Ryan swallow hard, as if his throat had now gone totally dry.

"For now," Mr. Collins said, "I'm not going to give you any grade at all."

"But this is my paper," Ryan said. "Friday was the deadline."

"Well," Mr. Collins said, "there's a new deadline for you. Next Wednesday, before Christmas break."

"I have to do the whole paper over?" Ryan said.

"You can start this one over, and actually put it in your own words *and* your own voice this time," he said. "Or you can pick another subject and start from scratch. Your call."

"I can't, Mr. C.!" Ryan said. "I could barely finish this one on time, even with Lucas helping me!"

"Yes, you can," Mr. Collins said. "I'm not looking for the students I think you should be. I want you to be the best student *you* can be. And that's going to start with you writing the best paper you can write. Alone."

Mr. Collins was leaning against the front of his desk now, hands behind him, the way he did in class sometimes.

"I know you're his friend, Lucas," Mr. Collins said. "But the right way for you to be his friend now is to let Ryan do his own work."

Here was somebody else, Lucas thought, talking about doing things the right way, even now that things had gone this wrong.

"You both clear on this?" Mr. Collins said.

"Yes, sir," Lucas said.

"Yes, sir," Ryan said.

Lucas thought his friend might cry. Lucas felt as if he'd just finished a pop quiz he hadn't known was coming. And wasn't sure he'd gotten all the answers right.

"If I were you, Ryan," Mr. Collins said, "I'd get out of here and get to work. "Lucas? You hang around for a minute, I want to have another word with you."

What now?

After Ryan had shut the door behind him, it was just Mr. C. and Lucas.

"I believe you were just trying to help out a friend you thought was in a bad spot," Mr. Collins said. "Except you do him no good if you do his work for him, even if you didn't see it that way, or even intend it that way. He really does have to do this himself, whatever kind of paper he turns in now, and whatever happens after we all get back from Christmas break."

"Okay," Lucas said.

"I know you were just trying to do a teammate a solid," Mr. Collins said. "But sometimes that can lead you to a bad decision, no matter how good your intentions were."

He wanted to tell Mr. Collins that it was Ryan who had really made the bad decision, by not putting in the extra work. But he didn't. Trying to be a solid teammate to the end.

"Glad you gave both of us a second chance," Lucas said.

For the first time, Mr. Collins smiled.

"If I didn't," he said, "I wouldn't be the guy you wrote about in your own paper."

"How'd I do?" Lucas said.

"You'll find out your grade along with everybody else after break," Mr. C. said.

"I feel a little bit like I got an F in here today," Lucas said.

"Let's call it an incomplete grade for now," Mr. Collins said.

"But if Ryan messes up on *this* paper now and gets a lousy grade, I feel like that's partially going to be on me," Lucas said.

"You know that commercial on TV where they say that life comes at you fast?" Mr. Collins said. "It happens all the time in our own lives when other people's choices affect ours."

Do they ever, Lucas thought.

Man, do they ever.

"You look like you want to say something," Mr. Collins said.

There was a lot Lucas wanted to say. But he felt as if everybody had said enough today. He just stood up, shook Mr. C.'s hand, thanked him again for giving Ryan a do-over, and walked out of the classroom.

Ryan was waiting for him in the hall.

"You still have to help me," he whispered to Lucas.

As low as Ryan had kept his voice, Lucas's head still whipped around, afraid that Mr. Collins had followed him out of the classroom and had somehow heard.

But it was just the two of them.

"I can't," Lucas said. "You just heard Mr. C. tell me not to."

"He doesn't have to know," Ryan said. "No one has to know."

"I'd know," Lucas said.

TWENTY-SEVEN

Ryan, who loved to eat, ate quickly at lunch the next day, telling Lucas and Maria that he had to get to the library and do some work.

"Ryan?" Maria said. "Ryan *Moretti*? Bolting from the cafeteria to do *schoolwork*?" She smiled at Lucas. It was one of those smiles that made it difficult for Lucas to focus on what she was saying. "Who *was* that?"

"Turned out Mr. C. gave him a little extra time to work on his paper," Lucas said.

"I thought he passed his in along with the rest of us," she said.

"He thought he was done," Lucas said. "It just turned out he wasn't *done* done."

He quickly changed the subject back to basketball. Even when he was with Maria, basketball always made him felt as if he was on safe, and solid, ground.

"I can't believe we only have one more game before Christmas," he said. "And the way we're playing, I'm worried that even taking one Saturday off will slow our roll."

Maria giggled.

"Did you actually just say 'slow our roll'?" she said.

"I heard Stephen Curry say it after a Thunder game the other night," Lucas said, suddenly feeling sheepish. It happened a lot in her presence, even though being with her was another way of being on safe, solid ground.

"Stephen Curry is allowed to say it," she said. "You are not."

"Now you're the one slowing *my* roll," Lucas said.

She laughed. So did Lucas. It felt good. When they were walking back to class, it occurred to him that he hadn't thought about Gramps once during lunch.

It still happened that way sometimes.

Just not very often.

The last game before Christmas was against the Jefferson Jazz at Claremont Middle.

Even Christmas felt different this year. He was still excited about it. He still loved this time of year. But it was different, the way a lot of things were.

Gramps still wasn't having dinner with them. He never stopped by the house. He didn't pick up Lucas for practice or drop him off after.

He was Lucas's coach. He was the coach and Lucas was one of his players. *That* was their relationship, in the gym and at these games, which were starting to feel bigger and bigger as the Wolves kept winning.

No game felt bigger, at least so far, than the one against the Jazz. They were undefeated too. They had a great point guard, a kid tall enough to play center named Corey Tanner. Lucas remembered Corey—all too well—from sixth-grade ball. The Jazz had just missed making the playoffs last year. So the Wolves had only played them once. It hadn't been pretty for Lucas, even though the Wolves had ended up winning by a point. It was the one time last season when he'd felt totally dominated by the guy he was matched up against.

"He's a bigger version of me," Lucas was saying to Billy while they warmed up. "Taller and better."

"No," Billy said. "He's just taller."

"I still can't get last year's game out of my brain," Lucas said.

"He shot over me every time he wanted to. I couldn't get my shot over him."

Ryan came by and heard them. "Today's a do-over," he said. "Like my paper."

"Thought we weren't going to talk about that," Lucas said.

"We're not," Ryan said.

They actually hadn't been talking about the paper, once Lucas had told Ryan that he couldn't help him this time around. Lucas didn't even know if Ryan had stayed with his tennis coach as his subject, or picked another one. He'd have to wait to find out.

"All I want to talk about today," Lucas said, "is acing this test against the Jazz."

It turned out to be one of those great days. Everybody brought their A games. Corey was as good as Lucas remembered, and just as long and athletic. But Lucas and Ryan were running their pick-and-rolls so well that Ryan kept getting open, either to drive the ball to the basket or on what Gramps liked to call the pick-and-pop. When Corey would switch on Ryan and Max Barrett, who had been guarding Ryan, would end up on Lucas, Lucas would make him pay. Max was just as long as Corey, but not nearly as quick. Lucas stepped back for a couple long jumpers, and drove by him a couple times in the first half.

At the other end, Ryan was helping Lucas out on Corey every

chance he got. Corey was still knocking down shots. Just not the way he had last season. The Wolves ran every chance they got. The Jazz did the same. At halftime the score was 30–30, the most total points in a Wolves game all year. Going into the fourth quarter, the game was still tied at 42.

The Jazz finally went to a zone as a way of trying to attack the way the Wolves were moving the ball and spacing the court and making their shots, especially inside. The zone worked. Suddenly the Wolves weren't getting as many easy points, because of the way the Jazz were packing the middle.

At the other end, Corey began to dominate Lucas the way he had when they were in the sixth grade.

The Jazz coach kept isolating Corey on Lucas, on one side of the court or the other. Corey kept backing Lucas in, backing him in a little more, getting to where he wanted on the court, then shooting over him.

Just like last year.

Lucas tried to overplay. He took chances on steals. Corey kept scoring. The Jazz got up six points with four minutes to play. Corey stepped back on Lucas and made a three-pointer. They were up nine.

Gramps called time.

"We're fine," he said.

"We're not fine!" Lucas said, louder than he meant. He wasn't

mad at Gramps today. He was mad at himself. "I can't guard that guy," he said.

"You did pretty well until the last few minutes," Gramps said.

"It doesn't matter," Lucas said. "He's killing us. Please put somebody else on him."

Gramps ignored him. He turned to Ryan and Richard and Billy and Sharif. "Let's try our half-court trap on D," he said. "Ryan and Billy, you run at the guy with the ball as soon as he's over the line."

The ref blew his whistle. The other four Wolves players in the game headed back on the court. Lucas started to follow them.

Gramps gently put a hand on his arm.

"Sam," the ref said. "Time-out's over."

"One second," he said. "Talking to my grandson."

He knelt down in front of Lucas. Lucas could see it took some effort, and could see the pain on his face. He kept his voice low.

"You may not like it," he said, "but you've still got a lot of me in you. A big part of it better be that you're not a quitter, because I sure as heck never was. Only, you sounded like a quitter just now." He held up a finger, as a way of letting the ref know that the conference with Lucas was ending. "I'll take you off that big kid, if that's what you want. But if I do,

I'm taking you out of this game. Is *that* what you want?"

"No," Lucas said.

"You're the one getting knocked down right now," he said. "Now it's your turn to show some rope and get yourself back up."

Lucas didn't say another word. He just nodded. He went back to join his teammates. It was Wolves ball. Lucas got away from Corey, looked as if he might drive to the right, but whirled suddenly and threw a bullet of a crosscourt pass to Ryan.

Ryan didn't hesitate, just stepped back from Max and made a three.

The Wolves were down six.

Corey threw the ball ahead to Max, but Ryan and Billy swallowed him up on a trap. Ryan took the ball away, cleanly, drove the court, laid the ball in.

They were down four.

Two minutes left.

Corey beat the trap, started backing Lucas down again, on the left side. But this time Lucas didn't just hold his ground. He read the rhythm of Corey's dribbling perfectly, reached in at the perfect moment, knocked the ball away from him. Sharif grabbed it at the free-throw line. Almost without looking, he threw the ball down the court like a football quarterback, hitting Billy right in stride. Billy was the one making a layup now.

They were down a basket.

Twenty seconds left, the game tied, the Wolves ended up with the ball after Corey missed a wide-open jumper. Ryan got the rebound. Lucas brought the ball up. Gramps didn't call a time-out. He just signaled for them to play.

Lucas and Ryan tried to run one more pick-and-roll. But Corey and Max were ready for it. Max blew up the screen. Corey stayed on Lucas. Ryan had no clear path to the basket.

Six seconds.

Five.

Lucas knew he was outside his range. Corey was right up on him. But there was no choice but to put the ball up.

He stepped back, the way Steph Curry did.

He got the ball up and over Corey's outstretched arms. Lucas used all the strength he had in him to do that, actually ending up on the floor after he released the ball.

He was sitting on the floor, leaning around Corey to see, when he saw the ball go through the net.

Wolves 57, Jazz 55.

One last time, Lucas got up.

The next day, Gramps got knocked down again.

TWENTY-EIGHT

Nearly sixty years later, there was another story about the Ocean State Bisons in the *Los Angeles Times*.

Lucas's mom was the one who told him, because the story had popped up on her phone. Without telling him, she had been doing some research of her own about Gramps and his teammates and the scandal, trying to find out if there really was more to the story. So she had set a Google alert. If there was a mention anywhere about the Bisons, she found out about it right away.

She got the alert on Gramps on Sunday morning.

The story wasn't really about him. It was really about Tommy Angelo, who was eighty years old by now and close to dying.

"He's living in an assisted living facility outside Los Angeles," Julia told Lucas after she'd read the story. "It's where elderly people who can't take care of themselves on their own end up."

Somehow the reporter had found Tommy Angelo through his wife. She sat in on the interview, because Tommy didn't remember things as well as he once had. But the story talked about what he had done when he was at Ocean State, how he'd been the player who ended up in prison along with a couple of the gamblers involved, what he'd done with his life after prison, finally ending up working as a church custodian. The story also mentioned that two players who'd taken money to manipulate the point spreads, had died a long time ago.

Lucas's mom showed him the story. Lucas read it, and saw that in the middle, the reporter mentioned that a fourth player, Joe Samuels, was now living in Claremont, having changed his name to Sam Winston.

Mr. Winston, it said in the story, had declined to be interviewed about what the players had done, and the life he'd led since Ocean State.

"It was all my fault," Tommy Angelo said down near the

bottom of the story in the *Times*. "But they never forgave me."

Lucas and his mom sat at the kitchen table. After Lucas had finished reading, he read it again.

"He never said anything to me about getting a call from a reporter," Lucas's mom said. "What about you?"

"I would've told you," Lucas said.

She closed her laptop. Lucas imagined her shutting a door by doing that, making the story just go away. But he knew that wasn't happening.

"Do you think Gramps knows about this?" Lucas said.

"Maybe the reporter gave him a heads-up," his mom said, "and gave him one more chance to comment."

"But he might not know," Lucas said.

"He certainly won't know by seeing a story online," she said. "The only paper he reads is the Claremont *Telegraph*, and only when it's in his hands."

"He's going to find out," Lucas said.

She blew out some air, loudly, and ran a hand through her long hair.

"I'm afraid everybody is about to find out," she said.

Lucas's phone blew up for the rest of the day, but he didn't answer any of the calls, or return any, not even the ones from Maria. His mom had been right, of course. By the time he was back in school the next day, everybody knew. His classmates knew. His teammates knew. So did their parents. He felt as if the whole world knew.

So did Gramps's paper, the *Telegraph*. They ran a story of their own about the one in the *Los Angeles Times*. And the news that Gramps had wanted to stay buried in the past was bigger than ever.

TWENTY-NINE

tried to text you a bunch of times yesterday," Ryan said as they were walking to their first class.

"I know."

"You didn't hit me back."

"I didn't hit anybody back," Lucas said, "even though I did feel like hitting *something* a few times."

"So is it true?"

"It's true," Lucas said.

He hadn't taken the bus today. His mom had driven him to school, so they could talk one last time about all the questions he was going to get, the way she was sure his friends were going to react, how he should handle it.

"You can't hide from this," she said.

"I'm not hiding," he said.

"And you have to remember, you didn't do anything," she said.

Lucas answered her by quoting Mr. Collins, who'd told him that sometimes other people's choices affected your own, whether you liked it or not.

They had tried calling Gramps all day Sunday. They had driven over to his apartment and rung his doorbell. Nobody had answered. His car wasn't in its usual parking space on the side of his building. Lucas's mom told him that as soon as she dropped him at school, she was going to take another ride back over there.

"Your grandfather really did all that wack stuff?" Ryan said. "And you didn't tell me?"

"It wasn't my place to tell anybody," he said. "He never told me until I found out."

"Usually you tell me everything," Ryan said.

Lucas managed to smile, if not for long. "No," he said. "Most of the time you tell *me* everything."

Ryan said, "My mom thinks this is going to be a big deal with the people who run town basketball."

It was something else Lucas had discussed with his mom, what the fallout might be with the Wolves.

"She thinks they might want another coach to finish the season," Ryan said.

"Does *she* want that?" Lucas said.

"She doesn't," Ryan said. "But she thinks they might fire him."

From his room after they'd had an early dinner, Lucas heard his mom on the telephone in the kitchen for nearly an hour. She wasn't a board member herself for Claremont Basketball. But she knew just about everybody who was.

When she finally was off the phone, she came up to his room.

"They were actually more reasonable than I thought they'd be, and a lot less hysterical," she said. "They all feel as if they got blindsided by this news."

"So what did they decide?" Lucas asked.

"They didn't decide, as a matter of fact. Just about everybody I spoke to mentioned that it's Christmas, and even if they do end up voting to fire Gramps, they don't want to do it during Christmas. And they'd all like to hear from him before they make a decision."

"Did anybody try to call him?"

"A bunch of them did. They did as well reaching him as we have," his mom said.

"Is Gramps still in Claremont, even?" Lucas said.

"Kiddo," she said. "Your guess is as good as mine."

She sat next to him on his bed and put an arm around him.

"But if he is still in town," she said, "isn't he supposed to be at your last practice *before* Christmas tomorrow night?"

"He said he wanted to have one last practice before our break even though there's no game next Saturday," Lucas said. "That was after the Jefferson game. He said he wanted to have us be together one more time before we went on vacation."

She kissed him and left his room, shutting his door behind her as she did.

Where was he?

What was he feeling, being in the newspaper like this all over again, like he was one more page in Lucas's dad's scrapbook?

Lucas was just finishing his homework when he heard the doorbell, and yelled to his mom that he'd get it. When he got downstairs and opened the door, he saw Ryan standing there.

"Sorry I didn't call first," Ryan said.

"No worries," Lucas said. "I just finished my homework."

"Wish I could say the same," Ryan said.

"You finish your paper?"

"No," Ryan said.

"Dude," Lucas said. "You know it's due the day after tomorrow, right?"

"You think I don't know that?" Ryan said.

They headed up to Lucas's room. As they passed his mom's room, they heard her say, "Hey, Ryan."

Ryan said, "Sorry about everything that's happened with Coach, Mrs. Winston."

"Not as sorry as we are," Lucas's mom said.

When they were inside Lucas's room, it was Ryan who closed the door. And got right to it.

"You have to help me finish my paper," he said.

"You know I can't do that," Lucas said.

Ryan sat at Lucas's desk. Lucas was on the bed, cross-legged.

"If you're really my friend, you'll do this," Ryan said.

"We already talked about this," Lucas said. "You know you have to do this on your own."

"I know what Mr. Collins said," Ryan said. "I want to know what you say."

"I can't help you," Lucas said, "not this time."

"If you don't," Ryan said, "I'm going to get a bad grade. And when I do, I'm off the team. You always say you'll do anything to help the team. Well, you can help the team now by keeping me on it."

"If I do what you want," Lucas said, "it won't just be us who know. Mr. C. will know."

"It won't be like last time," Ryan said. "I'll change things, I promise. Dude, I'm, like, begging you."

He thought Ryan might cry.

"I can't," Lucas said.

"You mean you won't," Ryan said.

"No," he said. "I can't. I thought I was being a good friend and a good teammate before. But all that did was get us both into trouble."

Ryan stood up. So did Lucas. They were only a couple feet away from each other, neither willing to back up.

"Fine," Ryan said. "Start getting used to the idea of passing somebody else the ball when we get back from break."

"You don't know that's going to happen," Lucas said.

"Yeah, I do," Ryan said. "I might not be much of a writer. But I can still read. I read my own paper before I came over here. And it still stinks."

"Maybe you should do a different paper," Lucas said. "There's still time."

"That's your brilliant idea?" Ryan said. "I should start all over again, with a different subject, with a little over a day to go? Yeah, that's gonna work."

Ryan shook his head. His face was red.

"This is your idea of being my friend?" Ryan said. "Seriously?"

And suddenly Gramps's voice was inside Lucas's head, telling him that character was something you showed even in an empty room. His bedroom wasn't empty, but in this moment he understood what Gramps had meant.

"I am your friend," Lucas said.

"You've got a funny way of showing it," Ryan said.

He turned and walked out of the room. Lucas heard Ryan saying good-bye to his mom. Then the sound of the front door closing.

Now he was alone in his bedroom. He was the one making a choice that affected somebody else. He just hoped it didn't cost him a friend. And a teammate.

But if he'd acted differently, he would have lost a lot more.

THIRTY

To Lucas's great surprise, after having not heard from him since the Wolves' last game, Gramps did show up at practice the next night.

He was moving slowly. He seemed to be limping even more than usual. He didn't joke around as much with the guys while they were shooting around, and said nothing at all to Lucas.

But he was there.

When they were finished with their warm-ups, he called the players out to where he was standing at mid court.

"Pretty sure you boys are old enough to have heard the

expression about an elephant in the room," he said. "Well, guess what? Tonight I'm that elephant. Except I'm not invisible, much as I'd like to be these days. I'm standing right here in front of you."

Neil was the one who spoke up first.

"Is it true about you, Mr. Winston?" he said. "What we read?"

"Yes, it is," Gramps said without hesitation. "That boy they wrote about in the newspaper, I used to be that boy."

"So you did those things?" Sharif said.

"I did," he said. "But it wasn't worse than what I *didn't* do, which was stop 'em from happening."

Billy raised a hand, as if they were all in class, and he were asking permission to speak.

"Are you sorry?" he said.

"Sorry for who I was," he said. "But it's a funny thing: I'm who I am now because of who I was."

There was a ball on the floor right in front of him. Gramps leaned down, groaning just a little as he did, picked it up, and rolled it around in his hands. Lucas thought there might even have been just a hint of a smile on his lips as he did.

"I'm sure you've got more questions than the ones you've asked," he said. "But this is probably the last time we're going to be together for a while. And just because there're no

MIKE LUPICA

guarantees in this world, it might be the last time we might ever be together."

Is he going to quit? Lucas thought.

He told me he didn't quit.

"My grandson Lucas here," he said, "he told me I'd been dishonest with him when he found out who I was, and what I'd done back there in college. And I suppose there's something to that."

He stopped talking then, and spun the ball on the index finger of his right hand.

"But since I made the terrible mistakes I made, I believe I've led an honest life," he said. "And I know I've been honest with you boys about what I believe makes you the best players you can be, and maybe even the best people."

He looked at them all now, one face at a time.

"So while I will apologize to all of you for what I did," he said, "I won't ever apologize for who I am."

He looked at their faces, one after another, all over again.

"I just want you all to know how proud I've been to be your coach," Gramps said.

He nodded. Lucas didn't say anything. Neither did any of the other Claremont Wolves.

"Now let's play some basketball," he said.

They did. When they were finished, after what Lucas thought

might have been the best practice game of the whole season, Gramps did drive him home. When they were in front of the house, he told him he was going away for a little bit, and didn't know when he'd be back.

"Where are you going?" Lucas said.

"It's like everything else, son," he said. "If I wanted you to know, I'd tell you."

Then he turned in the front seat and put his hand on Lucas's shoulder and said, "Merry Christmas," and smiled one more time.

Just not his Santa Claus smile.

THIRTY-ONE

Gramps was not back for Christmas.

It was just Lucas and his mom. She got him a new pair of Stephen Curry Under Armour sneakers that she told him to have broken in for the last few games of the season, or else. There were some new school clothes, too. And a Celtics hoodie. And two Chip Hilton books Lucas had never read.

Lucas used allowance money he'd saved up to buy a new picture frame that Maria helped him pick out. Inside it was a photograph he'd found in the attic, one of his dad and his mom from high school, Dad in his Claremont High uniform, his arm around her, both of them smiling, as if they really were going to live happily ever after, forever.

She cried when she unwrapped it.

"I told Maria this was going to happen," Lucas said.

"Good tears," she said. "We've talked about them before."

"I still don't believe good tears are a real thing," he said.

"Well, you're wrong," she said.

The Chens invited them for Christmas dinner. After dinner was over, Maria watched the second-to-last NBA game on television with Lucas and Neil before it was time for Lucas and his mom to leave.

When they were back home, Lucas said, "I can't ever remember having a Christmas without him."

They both knew who he was talking about.

"It's because you've never had one without him," she said.

"Where do you think he is?" Lucas said.

"I wish I knew," she said.

"You think he's gone for good?" he said.

"Even after everything that's happened," she said. "I don't thing he'd leave for good without saying good-bye."

It wasn't just Gramps who had disappeared. Ryan had done the same thing, pretty much. Lucas hadn't seen him, or talked to him since last Wednesday, when Ryan had delivered his paper to Mr. Collins.

Lucas had asked Ryan about the paper, but he said he didn't want to talk about it. When Lucas pressed him, and asked if he was happy with it, Ryan just said, "All that'll matter is if Mr. Collins is."

Then he'd sat by himself on the bus ride home. Maybe he was still angry at Lucas for not going against Mr. Collins's wishes, and helping him out. Maybe he was already expecting the worst when he got the paper back, and was already starting to blame Lucas if he didn't get to finish the season, as if somehow this was all Lucas's fault.

Somehow, in a season where his team hadn't lost a game, Lucas felt as if he'd lost Gramps and his best friend, too.

His two best friends.

Mrs. Moretti coached the first game back after Christmas, the Saturday before school would start up again. She said Gramps had called her the day before and told her that he wouldn't be able to make it back for the game.

"Did he say where he was calling from?" Lucas said.

"He did not," she said.

"Did he say when he might be back?" Lucas said.

She shook her head. "So you and your mom still haven't spoken to him?"

Now Lucas shook his head. "Have the people on the board

decided what to do about him when he does come back, if he does?"

"Nothing has changed," she said. "They want to talk to him before they make up their minds."

They were ten minutes from the start of their game against the Harkness Pelicans. Lucas had just taken his last warm-up shot, making one last three-pointer before he came over to the bench. The rest of the guys were still out there, including Ryan, who was at least talking to Lucas for the first time in over a week. Lucas could still feel some attitude from him. But they had a game to play. And to win.

Mrs. Moretti came over and sat down next to Lucas as he drank some Gatorade.

"I need you to be my assistant coach today," she said.

"You don't need me to do anything but play," he said.

She grinned. "I need a little more than that," she said. "Nobody knows this team better than you do, maybe with the exception of the coach who's not here today."

"You're here," Lucas said. "You got this."

"They used to call me a coach on the floor back in the day," she said. "But it's different when you're out there. So you see anything today you think we should be doing, you tell me, okay?"

Lucas grinned and bumped her some fist.

MIKE LUPICA

When Ryan got back to the bench he said, "What was all that between you and my mom?"

"She was just making me promise to throw you the ball every chance I get," Lucas said.

"She's always telling me she has a brilliant basketball mind," Ryan said. "That's just more proof of it."

Lucas nodded at him. "We good?" he said.

Ryan made a gesture with his hand that seemed to take in the whole gym, or maybe the day.

"We're always good in here," he said.

The Pelicans were the smallest team, across the board, they'd played all season. The Wolves had a size advantage at every single position, including point guard, where Lucas would be lined up against another kid he'd been playing against since fifth grade, Jamie Alderman. Jamie was at least a head shorter than Lucas. Maybe more than that. But Lucas knew there wasn't a quicker guard in the league, or a slicker handler of the ball. Lucas was proud of his own ability with the ball.

He also knew this about Jamie:

He had never thought being the smallest kid on the court was any kind of disadvantage.

"This is gonna be weird," Ryan said, right before it was time for him to inbound the ball to Lucas to start the game.

"Now that your mom is head coach?" Lucas said.

"Uh, *yeah*," Ryan said.

"We're fine," Lucas said, knowing he sounded like Gramps.

This time it was the Wolves jumping off to an early lead. As quick as Jamie was, he still couldn't manage to stay in front of Lucas on defense. And this week, Lucas was able to shoot over somebody the way Corey had been shooting over him in their last game. On top of all that, their pick-and-roll offense was working as well as it had all season. Today Lucas was the one getting the most open looks.

Sharif came out hot, too. Billy and Richard were controlling the boards. The Wolves were ahead by eight at the end of the first quarter, but Lucas thought they should have been ahead by more.

Mrs. Moretti gave him a quick rest at the start of the second quarter, replacing him with Neil. But the Wolves increased their lead with Lucas sitting right next to Ryan's mom on their bench.

"This might be the best Neil has looked all season," Mrs. Moretti said. "I don't want to ice you. But I'm thinking about leaving him in there."

"Your assistant coach for the day agrees with you," Lucas said.

When Lucas did get back in there, the Wolves increased their lead to twelve. He didn't want to get ahead of himself, he was big on staying in the moment, but he couldn't help but think that if they won today, they would already qualify for the championship game. Even if they lost one of their last regular-season games, they'd still only have one loss. The worst they could do was tie the Jazz for best record. And if they did end up tied, the Wolves would get home court in the championship game, because they'd beaten the Jazz.

But Lucas wanted to win them all. He'd come into the season thinking they could win all their games, even if he hadn't said that to Gramps or Ryan or anybody. Now, after everything that had happened, if they did win them all it was going to feel all that much sweeter, at least to him. Even if Gramps didn't get to share in the championship.

How would I feel about that, really?

How would I feel if Gramps didn't get to finish the season?

He shook his head, as if to keep his brain from wandering away from the task at hand.

Focus on winning the game today.

So much had changed across the season, but not that.

Mrs. Moretti went with their starters when it was time to start the second half. Before they went back out, she turned to Lucas and said, "Any words of wisdom from my assistant?"

"Yeah," he said. "Pedal to the metal."

"That's what my college coach always used to tell us," she said, "when he wasn't telling us to get our butts back on defense."

"More words of wisdom," Lucas said.

But then Ryan, who'd told Lucas before the game that things were going to feel weird today, was the one who turned weird. They were still leading by twelve, but Ryan acted as if the game had already turned into a blowout, and he didn't have to take the rest of it seriously.

Lucas knew how much his friend wanted to win, in basketball or tennis or anything else. But now he was goofing around, trying to show off, maybe because he thought he could get away with it with his mom coaching, even though he should have known better than that. And *been* better than that.

It was still happening. Lucas remembered a game earlier in the season when Liam's dad had asked Gramps why he thought his son had played so badly after doing so well the game before. Gramps had grinned and said, "Maybe because he's twelve?"

Only, Ryan was acting like a six-year-old, firing up shots from the outside, taking his time getting his own butt back on defense after he missed another shot. When he did get back into position, the guy he was supposed to be guarding—Alex Faried—was the one making shots, inside and outside.

Lucas thought about what Mike Breen had said that time, about how hard it was to turn momentum around. But suddenly the Pelicans were on a 12–2 rip. By the time Mrs. Moretti got Ryan out of there, it was a game again. A real one.

Lucas looked over to the bench and saw Mrs. Moretti giving her son a pretty good talking-to, even though he couldn't hear a word of what she was saying. But what he *hoped* she was saying was this:

Cut. It. Out.

Now.

The whole energy of the game had changed completely by then. If you had just gotten to the gym at the start of the second half, you would have thought for sure that the Pelicans— who had come into the game with three losses—were the top team in the league. They were no longer chasing the Wolves. The Wolves were chasing them.

The game was tied going into the fourth quarter. Mrs. Moretti put Ryan back into the game, but he still wasn't doing much on offense, good or bad. Sharif got hot all over again. Lucas posted up Jamie a couple times, and scored over him.

Really, their problem wasn't on offense. The problem was at the other end. Even though the Wolves had picked it up again on offense, Ryan still couldn't do a thing with Alex Faried. Alex was still getting to his favorite spots on the court. He was still getting to the basket when Ryan would come out and try to take his outside shot away. And when the Pelicans got out on the fast break, Alex was beating Ryan down the court.

With three minutes left, the Wolves were losing by five points when Mrs. Moretti elected to call their last time-out. Lucas looked over at Ryan in the huddle. His face was red, the way it would get sometimes when he was angry.

Before his mom could give them any instructions Ryan said, "Mom, I can't cover that guy. You have to let somebody else try, or I'm going to lose the game all by myself."

Mrs. Moretti didn't answer him right away.

Lucas did.

"No," he said.

He looked at Mrs. Moretti. She offered a nod of the head that perhaps only Lucas noticed.

You asked me to be your assistant coach, Lucas thought. *Well, here goes nothing.*

Lucas turned to look right at Ryan.

"If your mom takes you off Alex," he said, "she might as well just take you out of the game."

He knew exactly who he sounded like. He was basically using the same words that Gramps had used when Lucas was the one trying to beg off from guarding Corey.

Ryan's face got redder. He was breathing hard, as if the game has already started back up. But he didn't say anything. Lucas knew they didn't have much time left in the huddle, so he got right to it.

"Do you want to quit?" he said to his best friend.

"No," Ryan said.

Lucas took a step closer to him. Ryan was taller, but he felt in that moment as if they were nose-to-nose.

"Are you sure?"

"I'm sure."

"You did the most to get us into this mess," Lucas said. "Now you're going to get us out. Got it?"

"Got it."

Lucas turned and led the team back on the court. Before the ball was in play, he took one last look back at Mrs. Moretti, who smiled and shook a fist at him.

Ryan didn't quit. Nobody did. Lucas and Ryan ran a sweet pick-and-roll, the kind they'd been running all season. When Ryan got away from Alex, Lucas hit him with an even sweeter bounce pass. Ryan made the layup. At the other end the Pelicans tried to run some clock. They finally swung the ball to Alex, who stepped back from Ryan, creating space, probably sure he was going to hit one more jumper. But Ryan timed his move at him perfectly, moved in on him without fouling him, and blocked the shot cleanly.

And he didn't just block it, he directed the ball to Lucas,

who fed the ball up the court to Billy. But instead of driving the ball, he stopped and kicked the ball out to Sharif, who hit a wide-open three.

The game was tied.

Maybe this game was different. Maybe this time they *had* managed to turn the ocean liner back around.

Ryan got another stop against Alex. Richard made a short jumper for the Wolves. They were back ahead by a basket. Ryan managed to bottle up Alex in the corner. Lucas ran in there to double-team, stole the ball cleanly. Ryan took off. Lucas got himself out of traffic, threw the ball as far as he could, watched Ryan catch it in stride, and drive the rest of the way for a layup.

The Wolves were ahead by four. They ended up winning by four. After the horn sounded, Ryan made his way straight for Lucas, putting out his hand for a regulation handshake.

"Thank you," he said.

"You're the one who made most of the plays," Lucas said.

"I meant thank you for being my friend," Ryan said.

Before they left the gym, Lucas asked Ryan if he wanted to hang out later, feeling as if things were finally back to normal between them. Ryan said he couldn't even though he wanted to, he had schoolwork to do.

"Wait," Lucas said. "It's the end of break. Nobody has any work to do."

"Well, I do," Ryan said.

"Work on what?" Lucas said, but Ryan was already hustling to catch up with his mom.

Mr. Collins passed back their papers on Monday. Lucas was pleased to discover that he'd gotten an A. But that wasn't the shocker in English. The big news of the day was that Ryan Moretti had also gotten an A.

The bigger shocker was that Ryan had thrown out his old paper and picked a new subject, even at the last minute. He hadn't written about Mr. Nichols, his tennis coach. He'd written about Lucas, and how hard it was sometimes to understand what it took to be a good friend, and to count on your friends.

"When our game was over on Saturday," Ryan said, "I went home and e-mailed Mr. Collins and asked if I could add one more thing to my paper. That's the schoolwork I was talking about. He e-mailed me back and told me to go for it. So I wrote about what had happened in the fourth quarter against the Pelicans, and how I learned even more about friendship when I least expected it."

"Wow," Lucas said, because that's all he could think of to say.

"You got me to stop acting like an idiot," Ryan said. "It just happened in a game this time."

"But you came up with an awesome ending," Lucas said. "For our game and for your paper." Ryan shrugged.

"Isn't that what good writers are supposed to do?" he said.

Then he laughed. They both did.

THIRTY-TWO

They finished their regular season without losing a game, even if they had managed to lose their head coach along the way.

Gramps still wasn't back, and they still hadn't heard from him. Almost every day, Lucas asked his mom if they should be worried about him, now that he felt as if anger toward his grandfather *had* been replaced by concern.

His mom said no.

"He might be wounded by everything that has happened," she said. "And he is an elderly man. But he is still the toughest old bird I've ever met in my life. He'll just show up one of these days, and when he does, I believe he'll tell us where he's been and what he did, and why."

It was the Monday of what Lucas and Ryan and the guys were calling Championship Week, the way ESPN did when everybody was getting ready for the NCAA Tournament. On Saturday they were playing Corey Tanner and the Jazz for the title at Claremont Middle. Lucas knew there had been some talk about moving the game to the bigger gym at Claremont High School. But when Mrs. Moretti asked Lucas and his teammates what they thought, they were unanimous in telling her that they wanted to play the game where they'd played their other home games this season.

"We earned home court," Lucas said. "And we want to *stay* on our home court."

This was before practice on Monday night. Their last practice before the Jefferson game would be on Thursday night.

On Tuesday night, just as Lucas's mom had predicted, Gramps just showed up right before dinner.

And proceeded to tell them where he'd been, and what he'd been doing.

And why.

He was wearing his old Celtics cap, but took it off when it was time to sit down and eat turkey meatloaf. It was then that

Lucas discovered that Gramps had called his mom that afternoon to tell him he was back, and hoped he could still invite himself over for dinner.

She had reminded him that no invitation was required, now or ever, and that she was going to let him surprise Lucas.

"He's been worried about you," Lucas's mom told him.

"In the whole crazy scheme of things," he'd said, "I think that might actually be a good thing for me, if not for him."

Julia told him she agreed.

Lucas asked him where he'd been.

"I went out to California to sit with Tommy Angelo before he died," Gramps said.

"So he's gone?" Lucas's mom said.

"He is," Gramps said. "You know how sometimes they say it's a blessing when somebody passes? In his case, I believe it was, just because there wasn't a whole lot of Tommy left by the time I got with him."

The two of them hadn't exchanged a single word or correspondence, he said, since Gramps had changed his name and left California for the East Coast.

"In that story in the paper, he talked about how we never forgave him," Gramps said now. "Well, I never knew he *wanted* forgiving. He was just part of the life I'd left behind me."

"Did he recognize you?" Lucas said.

"I'm not sure he would have on his own," Gramps said. "But the first day when his wife brought me into his room, she said, 'An old friend is here to see you.' Then I pulled up a chair next to him and took his hand in mine and said, 'It's me. It's Joe.' I hadn't called myself that in sixty years."

Lucas's mom said, "In the newspaper it sounded like his memory wasn't very good."

"Sometimes it was, sometimes it wasn't," Gramps said. "He'd fade in and out. But the gaps he had, and some of them were pretty big ones, I'd try to fill in for him. I told him we didn't need to talk about all that happened. But he wanted to, with me helping him along. It was important to him that I know how sorry he was about what happened."

Gramps sighed. "But you know what ended up happening? We ended up talking more about the good times we had before those bad ones."

Lucas's mom smiled. "You're the one who's always said that one good memory in sports wipes out a whole boatload of bad ones."

"Sometimes we'd just sit there for a long while and neither one of us would say anything," Gramps said. "And you know what I got to thinking about in the quiet of that room? If all of it hadn't happened, even the way it did, then I really *wouldn't* have had the life I've had. I probably never would have met your grandmother, son. We wouldn't have had your dad, even if we didn't have him nearly long enough. And I never would have been blessed enough to have your mom in my life."

"Thank you," Lucas's mom said.

"You're welcome," he said.

Gramps turned and looked at Lucas now and said, "And I sure wouldn't have had you in my life."

Day after day, he said, he'd sit next to Tommy Angelo's bed. Sometimes Tommy's wife was there, sometimes not. Mostly it was just the two of them, with Gramps sharing most of the memories because Tommy wasn't able.

"When it was happening," Gramps said, "to all of us, you thought you'd never forget any of it. But by the end, Tommy had forgotten most of it. Which maybe was another blessing."

One day last week he was holding Tommy's hand when he closed his eyes, and the hand fell away, and Gramps knew he was gone.

He stayed around to help Tommy's wife with the funeral details. She asked him to speak at the funeral, but Gramps politely told her no.

"I told her I'd already said what I came out there to say," he said.

"What was that?" Lucas said to his grandfather.

"'I forgive you,'" Gramps said.

THIRTY-THREE

Lucas would try to explain it later to his mom, how the minute Gramps walked through the front door, he was so glad he was back, it wiped out so much of what had been ripping him up inside since his dad's letter had fallen out of that book.

He didn't know if that meant he'd forgiven him. But it was like Gramps said: When he'd found out about Ocean State, he thought he'd think about it every day for the rest of his own life.

Now he was just glad that his grandfather was safe. He was safe, and he was back.

Before he went to bed his mom would say, "Priorities have a way of changing, kiddo. And can I tell you something? It won't be the last time that happens to you."

Before Gramps left, Lucas had tried to catch him up on what had happened with the Wolves while he'd been gone. The big thing, he said, was that he wouldn't let Ryan quit against the Pelicans.

"Sometimes a good teammate has to tell somebody something they don't want to hear," Gramps said.

"Or maybe tell a teammate something the man had waited sixty years to hear," Lucas's mom said.

"You want to know the truth?" Gramps said to both of them. "Telling Tommy I forgave him was more important for me to say than for him to hear, if you can believe it."

"I can believe it," Lucas said.

Then he asked his grandfather if he wanted to coach the Wolves in the championship game.

"Sounds like you boys did just fine without me," Gramps said.

"You always say what's right is right," Lucas told him. "It would be right for you to coach."

"Probably doesn't matter what we think is right," Gramps said. "I figure they don't want me. I figure they were just waiting for me to come back, if I came back, so they could tell me to my face that I was fired."

They were standing by the front door by then. Gramps had his coat on, and his Celtics cap back on his head.

"But if they don't fire you," Lucas said, "you'd want to coach, wouldn't you?"

"Would *you* want me to?" Gramps said.

The word was out of his mouth before Lucas knew it, almost as if it came out on its own.

"Yes," he said.

"Guess that's something I've been waiting to hear," he said.

"They still might want to let you go, Sam," Julia said.

"Not like I haven't been let go before," he said.

"But you're not quitting," Lucas said.

"I told you before," his grandfather said. "I might screw up all over the place. But I don't quit."

He put his hand on the doorknob and started to open it, and then stopped, as if one last thing had occurred to him.

"You ever wonder how I came up with Winston as my new last name?" he said to Lucas and his mom.

"I've been meaning to ask you about that," Lucas's mom said.

"I borrowed it from old Winston Churchill," he said. "I know you think I only read up on basketball history, Lucas, but I like to read about all kinds of history. And what I know about Mr. Churchill is that he got knocked down plenty of times in his life, especially when he was young. But England couldn't keep the man down. If they had, he wouldn't have been around when they needed him to save the whole darn country during World War II."

Gramps winked at them then, and nodded.

"He said one time that he wore his defeats like medals," Gramps said. "Said he learned more from them than he ever did from his victories." He nodded again. "I always kind of liked that one," he said.

He walked out to his car. But a minute later, he came back.

"I've been meaning to ask this," he said. "But that letter your dad wrote—could I have it to keep?"

Lucas smiled. "You shouldn't even have had to ask."

He ran upstairs and got it out of the top drawer of his desk. When he came back down, he handed it to Gramps.

"This really does belong to you," Lucas said.

Gramps accepted it as if Lucas had just handed him a trophy.

"After all these years," Gramps said, "it finally got delivered."

Then he left.

As soon as he did, Lucas's mom got on the phone and called Mrs. Moretti and told her that Gramps was back in Claremont. Ryan's mom said she would call the other board members and tell them. An hour later, she called Lucas's mom back and told her there was going to be a board meeting, open to the public, the next night at Claremont Middle.

As soon as she told Lucas that, he went upstairs and started making some calls of his own.

THIRTY-FOUR

They held the meeting in the library.

They invited Gramps to attend. Mr. Dichard, the chairman of the board and Richard's dad, told everybody in the library that Sam Winston had declined the invitation, saying that he didn't feel the need to come to defend himself as if appearing at some kind of trial. But, Mr. Dichard said, he'd thanked them for offering him the opportunity.

"Sam said that we all know who he is," Mr. Dichard said, "even if we didn't know who he used to be."

Mr. Dichard was the president of the Claremont National

Bank, and had played high school basketball with Lucas's dad. He and Mrs. Moretti were the only parents of seventh-grade players on the board.

There were seven board members in all. They were the ones who would vote on whether or not Gramps got to coach in the championship game. A few of the other board members briefly spoke. They all agreed that not only shouldn't he coach the game, he shouldn't be allowed to coach at any level of Claremont town basketball ever again.

"I understand Sam's sentiments," Mr. Dichard said when it was time for him to give his opinion. "But without sounding too harsh, the fact is that Sam committed a crime against basketball, no matter how long ago that happened. And I frankly don't see as how someone like that should be teaching our kids values, about basketball or anything else."

Lucas and his mom were seated in the front of the library. Mrs. Moretti sat next to them. After Mr. Dichard finished his remarks, it was Jen Moretti's turn. She stood and addressed the other grown-ups in the room. And Lucas.

"I've played a lot of basketball in my life," she said. "I played some of it at a pretty high level, and when I got to UConn, I was lucky enough to play for Geno Auriemma, one of the greatest basketball coaches of all time, for men or for women. And I just want everybody in this room to understand something:

I would have my son, Ryan, play on a Sam Winston team any day of the week."

She paused and looked around the room.

"By the way?" she said. "Which one of us in this room didn't do something dumb when we were young?"

Mr. Dichard got back up. Lucas thought he looked more annoyed than he usually did, which was saying something. Lucas hadn't been around him all that much, but he'd been around him enough to think that Mr. Dichard went through life looking annoyed.

"Dumb is taking your parents' car out without permission, Jen," he said. "It's not conspiring to fix college basketball games."

Now Mr. Dichard was the one looking around the library.

"Does anyone else have anything to say?" he said. "Because if not, we should go ahead and vote."

Lucas felt his phone buzzing in his pocket, and smiled.

Just then the library doors opened, and the rest of the Claremont Wolves came walking in.

Now Lucas stood up.

"We've got something we'd like to say," he said.

THIRTY-FIVE

Sharif's dad had brought some of the guys in his van. Mrs. Chen had brought some, along with Maria, who'd told Lucas she wasn't missing this for anything. Billy's dad had brought the rest of the team.

The players stood in front of the library, as if they were getting ready to play a big game. In a way, that's exactly what they were doing.

Or maybe they were about to hold a board meeting of their own.

Lucas had thought about reading the speech he'd written the

night before. But he knew he didn't need notes. He knew what he wanted to say by heart. Maybe because he was speaking from the heart.

"Since my grandfather isn't here to speak for himself," Lucas said. "I guess it'll be okay for me to speak for him."

He looked at Mr. Dichard, who nodded, but didn't look very happy about it. Then Lucas gave a quick look at his mom. She just smiled. He'd told her his plan about his teammates the night before. He'd shown her his speech before they'd made the ride over here. After she read it, she told him that if he even changed a single word, he was grounded.

"It's an even better paper than you wrote for Mr. Collins, if you ask me," she'd said.

Lucas began by thanking all the board members for everything they did for their team, and all the other boys' and girls' teams in town basketball. He thanked his teammates for being there because, he said, that's what teammates did, they were always there for one another.

He thanked Mrs. Moretti for everything she'd done while Gramps had been away.

Lucas took a deep breath.

Time to get to it.

"What I really want to say, for myself and for my teammates, is that for everything the grown-ups have done for our team, it's still *our* team," he said. "If there's one thing my gramps has stressed over the last two seasons, it's that it's the players' game. And these games are *about* us, not you."

He had teammates on both sides of him. He looked to his left, then his right. Now they were the ones nodding approval.

"My grandfather is a huge part of our team," Lucas said. "We know that better than anybody in this room. We wouldn't be where we are, and who we are, without him. It's why all of us on this team don't think it should be up to you whether he finishes the season out, or not. We think it should be up to us. We're here because we think the ones who should get to vote tonight are us."

"Now hold on a second," Mr. Dichard said.

"No," Lucas's mom said, standing in the back of the room, "*you* hold on, Ed."

Lucas said to his teammates, "All those in favor of my gramps getting to coach the championship game, raise your hand."

One by one, in formation, the Claremont Wolves raised their hands.

Lucas raised his last. "There's one more thing I want to say."

He cleared his throat. He wished he had some water. Bad time to get dry throat.

"Nobody would ever say that my grandfather *didn't* make a huge mistake a long time ago, one he's regretted ever since.

But the last time he was with us, he talked to us about second chances. I heard Mr. Dichard talk about a crime before. Now I'm just a kid. But to me, the biggest crime would be if you all don't give my grandfather a second chance."

No one heard the door open again. The only one who saw Gramps standing in the back of the room was Lucas, because he was staring right at him.

They smiled at each other.

Now Lucas wasn't talking to the other grown-ups in the room, or to his teammates.

He was talking to Sam Winston.

"I kept thinking that my gramps was the one who owed me an apology when I found out what he did," Lucas said. "But I'm the one who owes him an apology. For not accepting his when he offered it to me."

He walked to the back of the room and hugged Gramps, who hugged him back. No one said anything in the library until Mr. Dichard did.

"I guess Lucas is right," he said. "One vote tonight is enough."

The Claremont Wolves cheered.

THIRTY-SIX

Gramps drove Lucas and Ryan to the big game on Saturday morning.

They were the first ones to the gym. It gave them a chance to work more on the help defense they'd practiced on Thursday night, as a way of getting ready to play the Jefferson Jazz, and particularly Corey Tanner.

"We're not gonna use this scheme of mine the whole game," Gramps said. "Who knows, maybe we won't need to use it at all if things go our way. But even if we just get one chance to use it, we better use it right, because the championship might ride on it."

Maybe because it was just the three of them for now, Gramps's voice sounded really loud in the gym, as if he were shouting, even though he never did that.

"By now," Gramps said to Lucas and Ryan, "I guess we've figured out that we can all use a little help sometimes."

They had rolled out bleachers on both sides of the gym for the championship game, as a way of accommodating the biggest crowd, by far, Lucas and the guys had seen all season.

The championship trophy was somewhere in the building. They didn't know where. But it was here, and so were they.

"Still a long way to go between us and that trophy," Lucas said to Ryan when they were in the layup line.

"Dude," Ryan said. "I'm just glad we're all here. Because it wasn't all that long ago that I wasn't sure I'd be."

"Or Gramps," Lucas said.

"You still keeping that basketball journal?" Ryan said.

Lucas told him it had turned into more of a project than their English papers, because of everything that kept happening.

"Let's go write a good ending," Ryan said.

"How about a great one?" Lucas said.

Not for the first time, he was glad Mr. Collins had suggested he keep a diary. Mr. C. had been right. Someday when he read it, he still might not believe everything that had happened, even though he'd lived it all.

When Gramps gathered them around him right before the start of the game, he kept his remarks brief. As usual.

"Everything under the sun that needs to be said has been said," Gramps told them. "I'll just build on something my grandson said the other night. You all know who you are. Now all that's left to do is show everybody one more time."

Lucas looked up into the bleachers behind their bench. His mom was sitting next to Maria and her parents. Even Maria's grandmother was there. At the end of the row was Mr. Collins, sitting next to Ryan's dad.

Corey Tanner was still getting his shots against Lucas in the first half. He just wasn't making as many as he had in the first half, the last time the Wolves had played the Jazz. And Lucas was using just about every defensive trick he knew to slow him down. He was overplaying when he could. He was picking him up full-court sometimes. He was willing to try anything to get him off his game, and away from his favorite spots.

And the Wolves were making Corey work as much as they could on defense, running one pick-and-roll after another. They didn't all result in baskets, of course. But they were working that play, working their stuff, the way they had all season, and working the other team's best offensive player as hard as they possibly could, looking to tire him out.

Gramps was running his players in and out, using his bench,

almost like a hockey coach sending his players over the boards for shorter shifts than usual, telling them he wanted everybody on the team to have fresh legs by the fourth quarter.

"You boys got the rest of the school year to get your rest," Gramps said during one time-out.

"What if we make the state tournament?" Ryan said.

Gramps turned and stared at him, as if a snake had just crawled out of one of Ryan's ears.

"What tournament?" he said. "All's we got is today. All's we *ever* got in sports is today."

Just like that, what felt like such a long season when they were starting out, had become a short season. Just like that, it was a two-point game with two minutes left in the fourth quarter.

And two minutes would feel like a long season all by themselves.

Corey came down against Lucas, and began backing him in on the left side. Lucas tried to force him toward the baseline, knowing he preferred wheeling to his left when he went up and into his shot.

Didn't work.

Corey scored over him.

The game was tied.

Lucas brought the ball up the court. He shot a look at Gramps.

"We're fine," Gramps said.

They passed the ball around on the outside until Ryan, who had made a couple three-pointers already in the second half, had a wide-open look from the right. This time he missed. But Billy fought off two of the Jazz big guys for a huge offensive rebound, then kicked the ball back outside to Lucas. They had a new shot clock. Ryan was back in the low blocks, and made a move toward the free-throw line, as if they were going to run another pick-and-roll. But then he stopped suddenly, and was spinning back toward the basket. Lucas had read him all the way. Sometimes you just know. Maybe because they knew each other's games so well.

Lucas lofted a pass over Max. Ryan banked his shot home.

They were ahead by two again.

Just over one minute left.

The Jazz didn't rush. Corey chose the right side now for his isolation against Lucas. He checked the clock over the basket. But this time he didn't try to back him in. This time when Lucas gave him just enough room, dared him to take a three in this situation, he did.

Made it.

The Jazz were ahead by one now, the first lead they'd had in the fourth quarter.

Fifty seconds left. Even if the Wolves scored and took

back the lead, there would still be plenty of time for the Jazz to take the last shot, maybe the dream shot that from Corey or Max or somebody else that would win the championship game.

Gramps didn't call time, even though he had a time-out in his pocket. He let his players play. It wasn't just who they were. It's who he was. With ten seconds left on the shot clock, Ryan came up and set one more screen. Lucas threw him the ball. Only he didn't use the screen now. He was the one popping out, to the foul line extended.

Ryan passed the ball back to him.

Lucas let his shot go.

It felt like money leaving his hands, as if he'd put a Steph Curry stroke on it.

But Corey Tanner got a piece of it, because of those long arms. Problem was, he got a piece of Lucas, too. The sound his hand made on Lucas's shooting hand sounded like a thunderclap in that moment. It was a clear foul. The ref didn't hesitate, and blew the whistle.

Two free throws coming.

If Lucas made them both, his team was back in front.

So here were the two free throws he'd thought he might have to make in a big moment—or even the biggest—all season long. Here was why he had stayed in the gym or in the park until he had made ten in a row, *making* himself knock down ten in a row.

Only he didn't need ten now.

Just two.

All his life, from the time he'd starting playing, he had prided himself on being a team player. But now he *was* the team. He was like Ryan in tennis, out there alone, nobody to whom he could pass the ball.

He knew how many people were watching. The sound of the crowd today had been louder than anything they'd heard all season. But nothing had changed, not really. He was alone at the line. Him. Ball. Basket.

He went through his routine. Took a deep breath. Visualized the ball going through the basket.

He made the first.

Game tied.

He went through his routine again, telling himself not to rush. Took one more deep breath.

Lucas made the second.

The Wolves were ahead by a point.

Fifteen seconds left in the big game.

The Jazz coach didn't call for a time-out, either. He let his players play, in the biggest moment of their season. There was no need for him to draw up a play, anyway. Everybody in the gym knew where the ball was going.

Corey Tanner.

He dribbled to the right. Lucas shadowed him.

Eight seconds.

Just the two of them on that side of the court as Corey started backing in.

It was here that Gramps did something he hadn't done one time all season.

He yelled at them.

Top of his voice.

"*Now!*"

Ryan came running, long arms in the air, just as Corey turned back around on Lucas and went into his shot.

Only it wasn't just Lucas on him.

Ryan was there, too, using his own long arms, making the clean block on Corey that Corey hadn't made on Lucas at the other end.

The ball didn't get close to the basket. It ended up in Billy's hands instead, as the horn sounded with the Wolves still ahead by a point.

THIRTY-SEVEN

The Wolves cheered for themselves as loud as they ever had. They were all together in a raucous scrum near the spot where Ryan had blocked Corey's shot, jumping up and down, some of them hugging each other, some of them pounding each other on the back, some of them just throwing their heads back and yelling to the top of the gym.

When Lucas finally broke away from the celebration, he walked over to where Gramps had been quietly watching them from in front of their bench, the Santa Claus smile finally back on his face, as if this were the Christmas he had missed this year.

"Like I told you," Gramps said to Lucas. "Everybody needs a helping hand sometimes."

A few minutes later, after it was announced by Mr. Dichard that Lucas and Ryan had been named co-MVPs of the championship game, they were standing on either side of Gramps at mid court, and Gramps said, "Little help here," one last time.

Then the three of them held up the championship trophy together.

MIKE LUPICA

is the author of multiple bestselling
books for young readers, including the
Home Team series, *QB 1, Heat, Travel
Team, Million-Dollar Throw*, and *The
Underdogs*. He has carved out a niche
as the sporting world's finest story-
teller. Mike lives in Connecticut with his
wife and their four children. When not
writing novels, he writes for *Daily News*
(New York) and is an award-winning
sports commentator. You can visit Mike
Lupica at MikeLupicaBooks.com.